Also by S. T. Underdahl

The Other Sister
Remember This

No Man's LAND

S.T. UNDERDAHL

flux™

Woodbury, Minnesota

TEEN

UND

First Edition
First Printing, 2012

Book design by Bob Gaul
Cover design by Adrienne Zimiga
Cover art: Young man © Jesus Cervantes/Shutterstock.com
        Cover photo retouch © John Blumen

Flux, an imprint of Llewellyn Worldwide Ltd.

Library of Congress Cataloging-in-Publication Data
Underdahl, S. T.
  No man's land/S.T. Underdahl.—First edition.
      pages cm
  Summary: When popular, successful Brian returns from Afghanistan after serving in the National Guard, everyone but his sixteen-year-old brother discounts his erratic behavior.
  ISBN 978-0-7387-3305-0
[1. Brothers—Fiction. 2. Post-traumatic stress disorder—Fiction. 3. Veterans—Fiction. 4. Afghan War, 2001—Fiction.] I. Title.
  PZ7.U413No 2012
  [Fic]—dc23

                                                  2012023467

                              Flux
                     Llewellyn Worldwide Ltd.
                      2143 Wooddale Drive
                    Woodbury, MN 55125-2989
                        www.fluxnow.com

              Printed in the United States of America

This book is dedicated to those who stand
shoulder to shoulder in defense of freedom,
the brave men and women of the
United States Armed Forces.

ONE

(CNN)—In his State of the Union address, President George W. Bush announced today that a mix of strikes from land-based Lancer, Spirit, and Stratofortress bombers, carrier-based Tomcat and Hornet fighters, and Tomahawk cruise missiles launched by both the U.S. and Britain has signaled the beginning of Operation Enduring Freedom–Afghanistan. Military objectives, as presented to the Joint Session of Congress, include "the destruction of terrorist training camps and infrastructure, the capture of Al Qaeda leaders, and the cessation of terrorist activities in Afghanistan..."

"Dammit, Dov, can you at least put your dirty clothes in the hamper *once in a while?*" Mom complains. Though I can't see her, the strained sound of her voice tells me she's bending down to gather a double armful of limp jeans and ratty socks from my bedroom floor. "You're sixteen; I shouldn't have to pick up after you. Don't you think I have more important things to worry about these days?" There's a *whomp* sound as she tosses the entire load out into the hallway.

"Sorry," I mutter from where I'm lying on my bed, my face buried in the pillow. I'm watching bursts of red and blue color bloom like fireworks in the darkness behind my eyelids.

No further comment from Mom aside from a few grunts of maternal annoyance, then silence. Just when I start to think she's left my room, the sudden sag of the mattress tells me she's sat down on the bed beside me. *Uh-oh.* Sure enough, a moment later I feel the light pressure of her hand on my back.

"Look, Dov," Mom sighs, patting my back tentatively. "I'm sorry to bite your head off. I know you're depressed. You're not the only one. Brian is ... well, he's very important to all of us."

My brother Brian is the last subject I want to discuss with Mom; it never ends well. I try to block out her voice by concentrating hard on breathing evenly, hoping she'll think I've fallen asleep. To add to the impression, I give a convincing full-body twitch, the kind that happens sometimes when a person is just dropping off.

If Mom notices she's lost her audience, she doesn't take the hint. "I can't believe that after all these years, the National Guard is still getting shipped off to Afghanistan ... I never should have allowed him to sign up," she murmurs. Despite the fact that she's addressing me, her tone is distant, as if she's talking to herself. This is typical; I'm no longer surprised when people act as if I'm not there. In fact, I mostly prefer it.

Just as I begin to wonder whether a little snore would be too obvious, Mom's hand drifts up to tenderly stroke my hair. At least it *feels* that way at first; a moment later, she makes a *kah* of disapproval. "This black is just awful," she informs me, back to her God-Dov-why-can't-you-be-a-normal-kid? voice. "Are you supposed to look like a character from one of those vampire movies? If I were in your shoes, I'd think about how you're going to get it back to its regular color before your father gets home this weekend. And a haircut wouldn't hurt either."

Since Mom once referred to my normal hair color as "dirty dishwater," I find it surprising that she doesn't prefer the Ebony Glow that Miranda helped me pick out. There's no denying it's long, and for good reason: I discovered I like peering through the dark curtain of my hair, hiding from the world and its haters. It completes the comforting illusion that I'm invisible.

The bed shifts abruptly as Mom gets to her feet. "Get the rest of this mess picked up before you go to bed tonight. You hear me, Dov?" she asks, a warning in her voice.

"Yeah," I say into the pillow. *FML.*

I wait until I can hear Mom's footsteps fade away down the hallway before I roll over onto my back to stare at the ceiling. I've managed not to wonder what Dad will have to say about my hair, but now that Mom has brought it up, I have no choice but to consider it. My father, Mick Howard, is an over-the-road truck driver, which means he often doesn't grace us with his presence for weeks at a time. If I actually sat down and did the math, I'd probably find that he's been physically present for about 15 percent of my natural life. He even missed my birth, which is when Mom took the opportunity to name me after some character from a book she read in high school. When Dad found out, he just about blew a gasket. "What kind of girly name is Dov?" I imagine him hollering. "He's gonna get the shit beat out of him."

"I like it," Mom would have told him. "You weren't here and they needed a name for the birth certificate, so I had to make the decision." *Just like always*, she probably added. And that, without a doubt, would have launched them into an argument that goes like this:

Dad (challengingly): "You want me to stop driving, Laura? Quit my job? Who's going to support us then, if you're so smart?"

Mom (unwisely): "I could get a job, same as you, Mick."

Dad (with a condescending chuckle): "So you think you can support a family of three ... actually *four* now? On what ... (mockingly) *tips?*"

Mom: (softly): "We could manage for a while, Mick. While you found something else, I mean. It would be nice if you were around more."

(Momentary pause while Dad works himself into a rage)

Dad (shouting): "You want me to flip burgers all day for minimum wage?! Is that what you think I should do?! After all the years I've put in on the road? I should just throw that away, is what you're saying?!"

Mom (crying): "I don't know *what* the answer is, Mick. I'm just saying…you're gone all the time. I need…"

Dad (interrupting): "Oh, *you* need? *You* need? It always comes back to that, doesn't it, Laura?! When do I get to say what *I* need for a change?…"

And so on and so on and so on. I've heard a billion different versions of this same argument over the last sixteen years, and it always ends exactly the same way: on Sunday afternoon, like clockwork, Dad packs his cooler, fires up the big blue Kenworth, and heads off toward the west or east or south…wherever the next load is waiting for him. Suffice to say, Dad doesn't have much patience for anyone's crap.

Least of all mine.

TWO

....

When I was old enough to start school, Mom actually did get a job, not that it changed anything much. She works as a receptionist in the law offices of Hooke, Burns & Miller, or as Dad calls them, "Hook, Line, and Sinker." The general idea, as I remember it, was that once she got a job she would be contributing enough money that Dad would be able to cut back and start running more local loads. It never happened, though, and over the years I think even Mom got the picture. Dad likes being away from home. He doesn't *want* to be any more a part of the family.

To be honest, as I've gotten older I've grown to prefer the times when Dad is on the road. When he's home, he mostly spends his time pacing around the house, snapping orders as if he's trying to make up for the time he's lost being a father. Early on, I learned that it was easier to disappear and avoid the whole scene; I was never patient like Brian when it came to listening to Dad's rambling monologues about weigh stations and log books and what a pain in the ass it is to haul livestock down into the southern states. Brian was just better at dealing with Dad in general, or at least that's what I convinced myself as I faded toward the nearest available doorway; he seemed less likely to irritate Dad by asking the wrong question or by not asking the right one. As for me, I was better at hiding in my room, losing myself in whatever was playing on my iPod.

When Brian made Longview High School's varsity lineup as a freshman running back, things actually did change. Unbeknownst to any of us, it turned out that Dad was a former football star himself, or at least that's how he recalled it. At any rate, it gave him something new to talk about. He started trying to make it home for most of Brian's games, and if he couldn't, he tuned in via the satellite radio he'd installed in his truck just so he could listen to the play-by-play. "Yessir, you remind me of myself, back in the day," Dad would say, throwing an arm roughly across Brian's shoulders. "A chip off the old block." I'd turn away so I wouldn't have to watch Brian wrestle with the conflicting feelings of happiness that Dad was finally proud of something he'd done and guilt about the fact that Dad's pride never extended to include me. At the end of the day, I was pretty sure I didn't really care. I mean, it's kind of hard to miss something you've never had.

Over the years, I've sunk so far beneath Dad's radar that he sometimes forgets I exist. I'm not kidding about this: I saw the question "*Who?*" flash across his face at the dinner table last fall, when Mom suggested he invite me along on the hunting trip he and Brian were planning. Besides Brian's football games, hunting is the only other thing Dad ranks above work. I've never understood why, but Brian pretends to love killing defenseless animals too.

"Oh," Dad grunted when he finally noticed me sitting across from him; I'd stopped picking at my food and was frozen in horror at Mom's proposal. An awkward silence hovered over the table as Dad gamely tried to wrap his mind around the idea. "Uh, well…Dov."

"You *should* come, Dov," Brian inserted from my left. "Maybe you'd like it."

Across the screen of my brain, a slow-mo movie began to play: an oversized bullet in slow-motion trajectory toward the head of an unsuspecting doe, grazing innocently. A moment later, the doe's head disintegrated in an explosion of blood and bone; even from my spot at the dinner table, I could smell her confusion and pain.

"No way," I mumbled, letting us all off the hook. "I mean, no thanks. I've, uh, got some stuff to do that weekend." While I avoided the disappointed look on Brian's face, it was hard to miss the relieved expression on Dad's.

Gradually, and imperceptibly, Brian and I had slipped into an acceptance of our respective roles. We were:

Brian Howard, starring as
"Master of the Universe"
Adapted from the epic novel *The Perfect Son*

—"Two thumbs up!" says Roger Ebert

—"I can't think of anyone who better embodies the spirit and integrity that Longview High... hell, that this country... needs!" raves President Barack Obama

and

Dov Howard, in the role of
"Boy Least Likely to Succeed"
Adapted from the comic book,
One Family's Disappointment

—"No surprises here" reports the Longview Herald

—"Dov Howard sucks" says Anonymous

Evidence for our roles could be found pretty much everywhere: Brian ran for 1,200 yards in his last season on Longview High's state champion gridiron team, while I passed gym every year by the skin of my teeth. Brian was elected Homecoming King and "Most Popular Guy" in the senior class, while my friends consisted of a handful of messed-up emo kids like me. After graduation, my brother got engaged to his incredibly hot girlfriend, Victoria Hart, the only daughter of Longview's mayor; meanwhile, I was in the second year of being half in love with my art teacher, Ms. Twohey. And finally, like the perfect son he was, Brian joined the National Guard to pay for college. I, on the other hand, planned to spare my parents the expense by not going at all. That one would be easy; art was the only class where my grade was consistently above a C.

You might think it would be easy to resent a brother like that, but I don't. That's the thing about Brian; he's impossible to hate. Everyone who knows Brian knows he's the definition of awesome, and I, the kid who's spent his entire life in Brian's shadow, knows my brother's greatness is real. I've never met anyone else who affects people the way Brian does: just being in his orbit leaves you feeling somehow slightly improved because of it.

Here's an example of the kind of brother Brian was to me: when I was turning twelve, I asked Mom for a corn snake for my birthday. My friend Ali had one and it was the most awesome pet I'd ever seen. Mom was even considering it until I made the fatal error of mentioning that Ali's snake had gotten out of its enclosure and gone missing for a week (my point being that the thing was so durable that it turned up unharmed). After that, all discussion was over: no amount of begging, cajoling, or even (I'm now embarrassed to admit) crying would change her mind. I went to bed on the eve of my birthday knowing that no snake, corn or otherwise, would ever cross the threshold of the Howard home.

On the morning of my birthday, a jabbing pain in my shoulder woke me up. When I opened my eyes, I saw Brian standing next to my bed, poking me repeatedly and painfully with one finger. "Wake up, little birthday moron," he ordered. "It's time to get your present from the most awesome-est brother ever."

"Wuh?"

"Check it out," he told me, gesturing grandly across the room toward my dresser. The model of Hogwarts that I'd constructed out of Legos was missing, and in its place was an aquarium.

"No way," I breathed, hardly daring to hope. "No way, no way, no way..." I threw back the blankets and scrambled out of bed.

"Uh...*way*." Brian grinned.

And it was true: warming itself on a heated rock was a baby gecko. "That's so awesome," I breathed, suddenly and completely forgetting that I had ever wanted a corn snake. This was way better than a corn snake. I was heading for the door to call Ali when suddenly it hit me. "Wait," I said, "Mom. She'll never go for this." The realization that I wouldn't be able to keep my present hit me so hard I sat down on my bed.

"Don't worry, kid," Brian told me confidently. He lifted up a pinkie and made a winding motion around it. "I can handle Mom." And he did; before the end of the day, Mom had reluctantly agreed that Leo seemed harmless enough and deserved a trial period in the Howard household. "But I'm warning you, Dov..." she added. "If he gets out of that aquarium even *one* time..."

And that's how, thanks to Brian, Leo became the best pet I've ever had.

That's why we, along with everyone else in Longview, totally freaked when we got word that Brian's National Guard unit was getting sent to Afghanistan. He was assigned to a peacekeeping mission over there, something I'd never heard about before. Although "peacekeeping" might sound reassuring, it seems like every day for ten years there's been a report in the newspaper or on television that ends with the words "making today one of the deadliest days for American troops since…" This means that even peacekeepers like Brian are getting killed on a regular basis.

After his unit shipped out, Mom didn't come out of her room for three days and Dad took a load that kept him on the road for a solid month. Even I didn't know what to do with myself; I kept finding myself wandering down to Brian's old room in the basement to listen to LPs on the vintage record player Victoria gave him as a graduation gift. Finally I brought it up to my room; I don't think Brian would mind, and it feels good to have a piece of him nearby.

Amidst all our concern for Brian, I can't help wondering whether my parents, and basically everyone else, is thinking the same thing I am: what a shame that Brian, the *good* son, was the one sent off into harm's way. What if something actually happens to him? Dov Howard…the dud, the loser, the *anti-Brian*…will be a pretty lousy consolation prize. I'm pretty sure we can all agree on that.

THREE

....

My eyes open long before my alarm goes off, something that has been happening a lot lately. It's too early to get up for school, so I reach for my headphones; starting any day listening to Dashboard Confessional always puts me in an intensely reflective mood, which can be either a good or bad thing. Since the day hasn't officially started, I figure I'll chance it.

Most people have the wrong idea about emo kids and our whole scene; they think we're just a bunch of depressed teenagers in shattered hair, skinny jeans, and tight T-shirts who sit around cutting ourselves. Since Miranda, Ali, Koby, and I represent the emo contingent at Longview High, I'm probably qualified to tell you that's totally not us. We're not a bunch of sad-sack losers, just kids who like to hang out and listen to music that gets you thinking about how truly jacked up life is sometimes.

That's not to say the *other* kids at Longview don't think we're losers; there are a few—Ray Sellers, for example—who make that pretty clear. Fortunately, we don't care: when we choose to give douche bags like Sellers any attention at all, it's only to laugh about how ignorant and boring they are, and how much we'd despise ourselves if we were them.

Don't get me wrong; it's not that my friends and I are secretly living the lives of the rich and famous. No, we pretty much all have our FML moments, sometimes even all of us at the same time. Miranda's one of the sweetest chicks I know, but she's grown up in foster care and I've seen her cry more than once about her situation. Since 9/11, Ali gets flack for being Arab, even though he was born in Ohio and his parents are both professors at the university in Longview. I'm not exactly sure what Koby's deal is, but he's always complaining about how the medication his shrink gives him makes his head hurt.

If you printed up our life histories and put them side by side, you might think the four of us would have nothing in common, but we connect in a way that's kind of hard to explain to anyone else. When I look at my three best friends, I know we're all lit from inside by the same tentative, flickering flame, one that at best feels beautiful and pure and at worst burns like a motherfucker. The way I see it, if you're going to hang out with other outcasts, at least find some who speak your lingo.

As I lie there, the lyrics from "A Plain Morning" make

me think of Brian, and I roll onto my side to stare across the dim room at the aquarium on my dresser. As if he can read my mind, Leo is looking back at me, his pointy little lizard chin pressed against the glass.

"Hey bud," I call softly. "What do you think Brian's doing right now?"

Well, considering the nine-hour time difference, Leo opines, *your brother is probably washing the dirt off his hands in preparation for dinner.*

"Yeah, I guess you're probably right." I hope it's something like that.

And while we're on the subject of cleanliness, Grasshopper, Leo continues, *I was just wondering what's happened to the maid service around this place? Not to put too fine a point on it, but I'm up to my knees in my own you-know-what...*

"Yeah, sorry... I know." It's been quite a while since I've cleaned Leo's aquarium. "I'll get to it after school today. I promise."

If geckos have eyebrows, Leo raises his archly to indicate he's heard that particular promise before.

I glance at the clock. The truth is, I probably *do* have time. "All right," I sigh, sitting up. "Hang on."

You'll probably laugh at the idea that a gecko is the sort of pet you can feel close to, but to tell the truth, I feel closer to Leo than to most anyone else. Maybe it's because he came into my life around the same time my brother started morphing into the family superstar, but whatever the reason, Leo is my homeboy. My room wouldn't be the same without the scratchy sound of his claws against the glass as he waves at me across the room, or the sight of him sitting motionless, watching an unsuspecting cricket before he springs into action. Plus, Leo is always good for giving advice when the going gets tough, as it sometimes does.

Geckos are ridiculously fast and have great eyesight, so it's always a challenge to catch Leo for housecleaning. It's important to be careful, too; the first time I cleaned out Leo's enclosure, I grabbed him by the tail, then freaked out when it pulled right off in my hand where it wiggled away as if it were alive. The tail eventually grew back, shorter and a little crooked. I like the crooked tail better; there's something about it I can relate to.

Today Leo lets me catch him pretty easily, and doesn't even protest when I set him gently in the bottom of the fishbowl I keep nearby for cleaning days. He skitters over to the side and bumps his pointy head against the glass. *Don't be rearranging things,* he orders bossily. *You know how I hate change.*

"Too bad, so sad," I reply, moving his warming rock from one side of the aquarium to the other. "Gotta keep life interesting."

Hmph, Leo grumbles.

I shovel the damp bark, shredded newspaper, and weightless cricket carcasses off the bottom of the aquarium and into a plastic Family Mart grocery bag, then carry Leo's fiberglass cave to the bathroom where I rinse it in the sink and dry it on a bathroom towel, glancing first down the hallway to make sure Mom doesn't catch me. Her bedroom door is closed; probably still asleep, I figure. Mom sleeps a lot these days. Some days she doesn't even go to work, just spends the day sleeping.

"Hey ... get the hell out of here!" I hiss when I come back into my room and find Sheba, Mom's evil Siamese cat, staring up at the fishbowl from the floor below. "Git!" I aim a kick her way, causing her to disappear under the bed in a flash of silvery fur. Leo has been at the top of Sheba's must-eat list for years, and she never misses an opportunity to slink eel-like into my room to gaze longingly through the glass of his aquarium, trying to figure out an angle that would close the distance between them.

After I have everything back the way I want it, I pick up the fishbowl and lower it into the aquarium, then tilt it to the side so Leo can scramble out. He tumbles onto the fresh substrate, then heads over toward his cave. The feeder crickets live in a plastic box on a shelf over the aquarium; when I drop a couple into the aquarium they immediately scurry off, instinctively looking for cover. Drawn by the sudden movement, Leo's eyes swerve in their direction.

"Bon appétit, amigo," I tell Leo. With an eye on Sheba, I double check to make sure the aquarium's screen cover is securely attached.

Awfully international of you, Leo replies, belly-crawling after his breakfast. *But merci. And gracias.*

FOUR

....

Even with an early start to my day, I'm somehow running late by the time I get to school, which means I have to sprint through the dry October leaves from the parking lot to the main entrance of Longview High, the only door left unlocked after the first period warning bell sounds.

"You're late, kid," says Officer Mertz, tossing down his crossword puzzle as I come hurtling through the front doors and into the Commons. He's seated at his official post, a little folding table positioned between the school's main entrance and the indoor Commons where we eat lunch. From this vantage point, Mertz can see and therefore hassle anyone coming or going after the first bell. I figure it must feel like a real achievement to go through police training and end up guarding a table.

"Overslept," I mutter, glancing at the clock over the

office, which tells me I've missed the bell by only four minutes. Giving me a hard time hardly seems worth Mertz's energy, but maybe he's already screwed up the crossword puzzle.

"I should send you to the office," Mertz threatens. "Hit you with a detention. This isn't the first tardy for you, if memory serves me correctly."

Figuring there's no point in arguing with the truth, I busy myself writing my name and arrival time on the sign-in sheet next to his half-completed crossword. Sure enough, two of the answers he's filled in are scribbled out.

When I straighten up, Mertz is taking in my Ebony Glow, the *Bullet for My Valentine* T-shirt, my dark pegged jeans, and my Converse tennis shoes. It's times like this when hair that covers my eyes comes in especially handy: I instinctively know that any eye contact I give will be read as me being a smart-ass. Silence stretches between us; just when I think all is lost, Mertz gives a rumbling belch that suggests his breakfast included sausage and seems to instantly put him in a slightly improved mood. He reaches up and pulls a late pass from his pocket, glancing down at the sign-in sheet to make sure he spells my name correctly. "Howard?" he asks.

"Yeah."

"Howard," he repeats. "You related to Brian Howard?"

"Uh, yeah." *Great.* "He's my, uh, brother."

"Kid's in the Middle East, right?" Mertz still isn't writing.

"Mm-hmm." I wonder where this is going.

"Quite a kid, your brother. Remarkable football player."

Oh. Now I get it.

"Yeah. He sure is ... was ... is." I endure the customary 3.5 seconds during which Mertz considers the fact that I'm a far cry indeed from my brother, followed by the 4.7 seconds during which he wonders where my parents went wrong with me.

"So," he says, abruptly turning his attention back to the business of my tardiness. He seems embarrassed, as though he suspects I've been reading his thoughts. "Where was it you're headed?"

"Language Arts. Ms. Walker's room."

He writes me out a pass, which I take without thanking him. "Okay if I stop by my locker?" I ask, knowing I'm pushing it.

"Nope. I think you'd better head right to class."

I nod, bummed that I won't be able to take a detour past the art room. A glimpse of Ms. Twohey always starts my day out right, and this morning I could've really used it. With Mertz staring at me, however, I have no choice but to turn and begin the long walk toward the Language Arts wing, resigned to a day without sunshine.

I'm passing the main office when the door opens and a girl in a gray-and-black striped hoodie comes out onto the Commons. She's with Mr. Kerr, the school counselor. "Are you sure you don't want me to show you the way to your class?" he asks. "Longview's a pretty big school, you know. We don't want you to get lost on your first day here."

"No. I think I've got it," the girl tells him faintly. Her hair is dark and unevenly cut, the tips dyed red, as if dipped in blood. She glances my way and our eyes meet; her eyes are a pale slate color, like flat and icy behind her long bangs. She holds eye contact with me until I have to look away to calm down the weird *loop-de-loop* my stomach is doing.

"Dov Howard!" Mr. Kerr exclaims, as if I'm the answer to a riddle he's been carrying in his head all morning. "Where are *you* headed?"

"Language Arts," I tell him. "Mrs. Walker's class." Part of me wants to take another look at the freaky-eyed girl, but the rest of me is relieved to have a reason to look elsewhere.

"Great." Kerr nods. "Listen, Scarlett here needs to find Mr. Taylor's chemistry class. That's on your way, isn't it?"

He and I both know it is. "Yeah."

"Perhaps you can show her the way?" Kerr prompts. "To class?"

I risk another glance at the Ice Girl, but she's lost interest and is looking across the Commons as if the field of lunch tables holds great interest for her. "Sure," I agree.

Kerr grins and nods. "Thank you, Dov. That's terrific." Something about the way he's acting makes me think that Ice Princess makes him as nervous as she makes me.

"Terrific," she echoes now. It's not clear if she's insulting me or mocking Kerr, or both. Not that it matters, of course; my heart belongs to Ms. Twohey, so there's no reason I should care what this new girl thinks.

"I'm late already," I point out.

"Yes, you'd better go," agrees Kerr. "And welcome to Longview, Scarlett."

Scarlett doesn't reply, but keeps step beside me as we start walking. Out of the corner of my eye, I see that her nails are bitten down; what's left of them is painted black, like chips of charcoal.

"You just move here?" I ask, glancing at her sideways so as to avoid those piercing eyes.

"No," she says simply. "I'm only here for a little while. My grandparents live here. I'm staying with them."

I wait for more, but she doesn't offer anything, and we travel the rest of the way in silence. I suppose I could try harder, but I have my own problems besides making friends with the new kid.

When we reach the door to Taylor's class, I slow. "This is it," I tell her, "Mr. Taylor's chemistry class."

Scarlett sighs. I don't blame her; I'd be bummed too if I had Chemistry first period. Or, come to think of it, *any* period. I half-turn to look at her, ready to say goodbye, then see her swipe at her eyes with the sleeve of her sweatshirt.

"Hey," I say, "You okay?"

When she doesn't answer I reach out to touch her arm, but pull my hand back when she jerks away from me. "Yeah," she nods, her head down. "I'm okay. I'm fine."

I wonder whether it sounds as unconvincing to her as it does to me. "Look," I say, feeling bad I haven't been nicer, "I'll probably see you around, right? I mean, if you need, like, someone to hang out with ... "

"It's okay, Dov," Scarlett interrupts, finally looking up at me. I force myself to meet her eyes; she lines them in black like Miranda does, and when Scarlett reaches up to push her bangs absently out of the way I glimpse the dark eyebrows that wing above them. "I guess ... I kind of do better on my own. But thanks for walking me."

With that, she disappears into Mr. Taylor's room, leaving me standing in the hallway, wondering what just happened.

FIVE

....

Everyone convenes for lunch at our usual table in the Commons, unofficially "reserved" for us because no one else wants to sit with the freaky emo kids. Ali is already there when I carry my tray over and sit down.

"Sick shirt," I observe, indicating the *Hüsker Dü* T-shirt he's wearing. "Very old school."

Ali nods his acknowledgment over the carton of milk he's drinking. He and I have been friends since we both showed up in Mrs. Makovsky's second grade class at Phoenix Elementary. Even back in the grade school days, Ali was a kind of goth presence, showing up day after day dressed in a black T-shirt and sweatpants, vertical comb-marks clearly visible in his coarse, dark hair. When we hit middle school and most of us were trying to find where we fit in, Ali pretty much just stayed Ali, although eventually he traded the sweat pants for skinny black jeans. Idiots like Ray Sellers give him flack about the Middle Eastern thing, calling him Saddam and Haji, but Ali never seems annoyed by it beyond patiently reminding them he's Pakistani.

Unlike me, Ali's an only child and also unlike me, he's ridiculously smart. In fact, sometimes I wonder why he hangs out with us; the rest of us are grateful for C's while Ali quietly takes home report cards filled with A's. I'm not sure what he thinks, but to his credit, Ali never acts like we're his intellectual inferiors.

Ali and I are soon joined by the other members of our motley crew, Koby and Miranda. Even after five years, I haven't figured out what goes on in Koby's head under that mass of dirty blond hair. Most of the time he seems pretty much like the rest of us ... just another lost emo kid in skinny jeans and band shirts ... but then he goes through these periods where his mind seems to go into overdrive. When he's like that, his thoughts go crazy and his attention is all over the place. He might call me at three in the morning to talk about something that happened in gym class two years ago, or to describe an elaborate plan he has for winning the next season of *American Idol*. Shortly after that he'll usually drop off the radar for a few weeks—time we've all come to assume means he's probably in a hospital somewhere getting shock treatments or whatever they do to kids who go temporarily nuts. Then one day he'll show up again, back to the old, goofy Koby, and life just goes on. As weird as it might seem, none of us ever ask him about where he's been or what happened to him there. We're just glad he's back, and he seems to be too.

Miranda just sort of drifted into our group during freshman year. Unlike Koby, she does talk sometimes about what a screwed-up life she's had. Her parents were both drug addicts and she hasn't seen them since she was eight; she doesn't even know where they are anymore. "Probably a good thing," she added when she told me about it, but I heard the sadness in Miranda's voice as she said it. As messed up as my family is, I can't imagine being completely alone in the world.

Miranda and I both love to draw, but our styles are really different. Whereas my stuff ranges all over the place, Miranda draws only one thing: angels. She does something with the faces that's hard to describe, except to say that even though her angels have faces, you can't exactly see them. I remember once when Ms. Twohey asked her about it, and Miranda explained that her faceless angels were a metaphor for lack of hope. Our teacher looked like she didn't know what to say to that, but I kind of got what she meant.

Miranda's not a bad-looking girl; she's got that kind of red hair that's usually the kiss of death, but on her it actually looks pretty good, especially with her brown eyes. I'd never admit this to anyone, but sometimes when I look at her I think she might be even prettier than Ms. Twohey. While I'm confessing, I might as well tell you we made out once when Ali fell asleep while the three of us were watching the original *Halloween*. It wasn't something we really talked about afterwards, but Miranda does appear in my alone-time fantasies from time to time. Other than that, I remain firm in my devotion to Ms. Twohey.

Once Koby gets settled at the table, he immediately launches into an account of a show he saw with his cousin last weekend. It isn't uncommon for area bands to rent a venue and put together a lineup. Now Koby rattles off some of the bands on the ticket. "Tribes, These Hearts, The Suit. It was a *sick* show, man."

Ali sighs and looks at me sideways. "I'm bummed that we missed it. Too bad the Gator was out of commission."

"Hey, don't blame me," I protest. I'm the only one with a car, a green, needle-nosed station wagon we call the Gator, but one of the dash indicators had come on and I didn't want to risk driving it any distance until Dad took a look at it. "Unless somebody here knows what *Add. Cool.* means ... "

Miranda points at me. "I told you," she says. "Add Kool-Aid."

"Yeah, but grape or cherry?"

"Cherry," Koby says solemnly. "*Always* cherry."

"You know ... " I start to suggest that there's always the option of someone else asking to borrow their parents' car when my eyes fall on Scarlett in the lunch line and I lose my train of thought.

"We know what?" Ali asks when a couple seconds pass and I don't finish.

Miranda turns and follows my eyes across the room. "Oh," she sighs patiently. "Look, Dov ... I know it's hard for you to accept, but you're *never* going to get Ms. Twohey."

At the sound of my beloved's name, I turn to look at her. "What?"

Miranda has noticed something else. "Hey, who's that other chick?" she asks no one in particular. "In front of Twohey...the one with the sweet hair."

Everyone looks; I realize for the first time that Scarlett is in line in front of Ms. Twohey. I can't believe I didn't see Twohey standing there; this is truly a first.

"Some new kid," Koby supplies. "Sarah something. She was in my math class this morning."

"Her name's Scarlett," I correct, then feel Miranda turn and look at me, surprised. "Kerr made me show her where her class was this morning," I explain.

"She's hot," Ali says, an unusual observation coming from him.

We watch as Scarlett enters her student code into the lunch lady's keypad, then picks up her tray and starts scanning for a place to sit.

Without realizing what I'm doing, I lift my arm and signal, trying to catch her attention.

"Who are you, the Welcome Wagon?" Miranda mutters. Miranda's not big on surprises.

I watch as Scarlett sees me and then tries to figure out if she can pretend she didn't. In the end, she smiles faintly and slowly makes her way toward where we're sitting, but she doesn't bother trying to hide her resignation. As she grows near, I see that her lips are full and perfectly formed; suddenly, I wonder what it would feel like to smudge the pad of my thumb across them.

"Hey!" I say overly loudly, then gesture toward the empty seat at our table. "Sit here. There's room."

"'Nerds of a Feather' and all," Miranda mutters. I want to shoot her a scowl but feel like if I take my eyes off Scarlett's she'll slip away like water from under a stone. And for some strange reason, that's suddenly the last thing I want to happen.

Scarlett's blank expression causes me to wonder whether she even remembers me. "Dov Howard," I remind her, feeling stupid. "From this morning?"

"Yeah, I know. I remember."

"This is Koby," I say, pointing. "And Ali...Miranda. Everyone, this is Scarlett."

"You just move to Longview?" Ali asks.

Scarlett nods vaguely. She seems more interested in positioning her napkin in her lap.

As I begin to wonder how we're going to get through ten uncomfortable minutes before the end of our lunch period, the sound of my name comes over the PA system. *"Dov...Howard, please report to the office...Mr. Dov Howard, please report to the office."*

"Well, the FBI's finally caught up with you," Ali observes wryly. "I guess the system *does* work."

I barely hear him; my heart is too busy filling up my ears with blood. Even though kids get called to the office a million times a day for nothing more than a missing excuse slip, ever since Brian's been deployed, I imagine that if anything happens to him, I'll be called to the office to get the news. I even had a dream about it last week. Hearing my name announced from overhead now means I push back my chair and stand up on legs that are as flimsy and unpredictable as cooked spaghetti.

Miranda's breath is warm in my ear. "Want me to go with you?" she asks, leaning close. Her tone is casual, but the look in her eyes shows her concern. All my friends know how scared I am that something might happen to Brian while he's in Afghanistan.

I shake my head and try to smile. "I'm fine," I say, my lips dry. "Probably just won Student of the Week again."

"We'll get your tray," Miranda says, shooing me off. "Just go see what they want."

"Send us a postcard from the big house," Ali calls after me. "Write it on toilet paper if they let you have any."

As I stumble away from the table, my eyes barely register Scarlett regarding me with annoyance, likely over the fact that I'm leaving her alone with three people she barely knows.

Somehow I stumble numbly across the carpeted floor of the Commons and into the main office, where I find Mrs. Hoffer, the secretary, sitting behind the desk eating her lunch.

"I was called to come to the office?" I croak.

Mrs. Hoffer nods, holding up a finger as she finishes chewing, which seems to take forever. At last she swallows. "Yes, Dov. Your mother phoned. She had some car trouble on the way to work today and had to leave the car at the service station. She was wondering whether you could pick her up at work and take her back there, after you get out of school this afternoon.

"Pick her up at work?" I echo numbly, trying to force my mind to translate the meaningless words. "So it's not... Brian's all right?"

Mrs. Hoffer pauses on her way to another bite. "Brian?" she repeats, looking confused.

"My brother... I just..."

My knees give up and I sink down into one of the chairs positioned just inside the door of the office. They're usually occupied by students or parents waiting to see the principal, but for now they keep me from crumbling to the floor with relief.

"Oh my goodness, I'm sorry, Dov," Mrs. Hoffer apologizes, actually setting down her sandwich. "It never occurred to me that you would think... I'm so sorry," she says again.

"It's okay," I manage. "I—I just didn't know, that's all."

Mrs. Hoffer actually gets up and comes around the desk to sit down in the chair beside me. "Listen to me," she says, clasping her hands in front of her. "If *any*one can come back from something like that in one piece, it will be Brian. He's quite a guy, right?"

I nod, even though I doubt that Al Qaeda has much interest in Brian's remarkable yardage record, nor do I think that my brother has much chance to argue his greatness while dodging an insurgent missile.

By the time I manage to leave the office, the fifth period you're-gonna-be-late bell is ringing. I head back across the Commons toward our empty table, where I left my backpack. Grabbing it, I look at the place where Scarlett was sitting, wondering how things played out after I left.

31

Not that it matters, I tell myself. Being called to the office reminded me that I have bigger things to worry about than putting out the welcome mat for Scarlett WhatzHerProblem. A *lot* bigger things.

Things to Worry About
Something happening to Brian
Getting eaten by a bear
Something happening to Brian

Things that Don't Matter
Everything else

SIX

(**Los Angeles Times**)—*In a flurry of weekend press releases, the Department of Defense named another 12 U.S. soldiers killed in Afghanistan and related conflicts. These deaths bring the total killed since the beginning of Operation Enduring Freedom to . . .*

....

Amazingly, Mom and I manage to make it to the service station without a single argument. It turns out that the problem was only a loose hose. Normally, the added stress in her day would have pitched her right into a bad mood; she didn't see me before I left this morning, so when I picked her up I'd steeled myself for a laundry list of opinions about what I was wearing (*"For Pete's sake, Dov; you'd think those jeans were made for an eight-year-old girl"*); my hair (*"I'm making you an appointment before your father gets back to town this time, mister! And I don't want to hear another word about it!"*); or the general level of shame and embarrassment my existence brings to the family (*"Do you think I need my son looking like a messenger from the*

33

Underworld, Dov?") Instead, Mom is in a reasonably *good* mood; she'd even reached across the Gator's front seat as we drove to the station, rubbing a strand of my hair between her fingers and telling me it reminded her of a singer she likes on American Idol.

Mom's car is ready to go, so she follows me home. I'm hoping for a peaceful evening, but as soon as we walk into the house, things head south in a hurry. The blinking indicator on the phone says there are two messages: the first one is from Dad, reminding me that the lawn needs to be raked and mowed one last time before the cold weather hits. It's a chore I've been procrastinating, but when Mom shoots me a look, I know I'll be doing it tonight.

The second message is from Brian; at the sound of his voice, Mom takes a couple involuntary steps toward the phone and then freezes, listening with every cell of her body.

"*Hi guys!*" Brian says heartily from inside the answering machine; his voice sounds deeper than I remember, and something about his cheerfulness seems forced. "*Just wanted to let you know that it's hotter'n Hell here, but I'm still taking on oxygen. We've been doing training ops; sounds like we're heading off on a mission tomorrow. Hopefully something interesting, 'cuz it can get pretty boring here sometimes. Anyway ... I thought I'd catch you but maybe I got the time wrong. So anyway, I hope you're all good and Dov I hope you're behaving. I'll talk to you again sometimes soon ... love you guys lots! Miss you! Over and out!*"

A click ends the message, prompting Mom to make a

little sound of disappointment, halfway between a sigh and a sob.

"He sounds great," I offer. "Same old Brian."

"Yes," Mom agrees softly. "I just … I wish we'd been here when he called. Who knows when he'll have another chance?"

"He said 'soon,'" I point out.

Mom nods, but I can sense that her high spirits have slipped away. She doesn't even have to tell me to go out and get started on the lawn.

I spend the time while I rake, mow, and bag replaying Brian's message in my head. I wonder about the mission he mentioned, and vow for the hundredth time to Google "War in Afghanistan" in order to get a better idea of what's going on over there. I don't know why I haven't done it yet, except that part of me doesn't want to know.

By the time the yard's mowed and cleared of limp, clammy leaves, the streetlights have come on and my nose is freezing. My fingers are so cold I can barely do up the ties on the heavy plastic garbage bags. As I'm wrestling with the last one, a beat-up old car rounds the corner, slowing as it drives past. The passenger window slides down.

"Hey," calls a voice from the dark interior. "Hey … Howard!"

There's no mistaking the nasal voice of Ray Sellers, a kid who seems to grow more despicable with each passing year. From deeper inside the car, I can also hear the snickers and mutterings of Clayton Rozales and Josh Smith, who together with Ray make up what Miranda has dubbed the Idiot Posse. Aside from relentless harassment, and the mocking that often exposes how truly ignorant they are, Ray and his pals are harmless; still, my friends and I usually try to fly under their radar, which means that right now, I pretend to be deaf.

Unfortunately, Ray's pretending to be blind. "Whatcha doin', emo-boy?" he hollers.

"What does it look like?" I shrug, allowing the irritation I feel into my voice. I'm cold and tired, which means that Ray is an even bigger tool than usual.

Ray laughs his annoying, high-pitched laugh and revs the accelerator to make sure he has my attention. "I'll bet you wish your lawn was emo," he calls. "That way it could cut itself."

Wow, original. I've only heard that one about a thousand times.

The peanut gallery apparently hasn't; the car erupts into hysterical, idiot-worthy laughter. "God," Josh chokes, "that's awesome, dude."

"Yeah," Clayton agrees. "Awesome."

I should just ignore them, but something about how cold my face is makes it impossible. After a quick glance toward the house to make sure Mom isn't looking out the window, I raise a middle finger in salute.

This only sends them into fresh hilarity. Satisfied he's achieved what he wanted, Ray stamps on the accelerator so that the car shoots off down the street, fishtailing and spraying gravel behind it. Moments later, it's just a pair of red taillights growing smaller in the distance.

I push the mower back into its spot in the garage, hang up the rake, and drag the bags of clippings and leaves to the curb for tomorrow morning's trash pickup. Even though I'd been avoiding the chore, I have to admit that I feel a sense of accomplishment when I survey the yard, which looks flawless and uncluttered in the darkening evening. Inside, Mom has turned on the lights, making the house look bright and inviting. Standing outside in the chilly fall air, I experience a moment of intense appreciation for home. It makes me think about Brian and about Dad, about how differently I'm affected by their absences.

When I get inside, I'm pleasantly surprised by the sight of a pot of spaghetti boiling on the stove next to a pan of meat sauce. I give it a stir, inhaling the mouth-watering aroma of garlic bread that comes from the oven below. When Brian was still at home, Mom used to make dinner almost every night … I have many fond memories of pork chops with applesauce and stuffing, roasted chicken with couscous and peas, ham and scalloped potatoes … but since he's been gone, she rarely bothers to cook anymore. Mom and I are usually on our own for meals, which means I slap together a sandwich and Mom doesn't eat at all.

Tonight, though, two places are set at the table, complete with paper napkins. After all the physical labor outdoors, I'm starving, and the prospect of a hot, sit-down dinner fills my heart with joy. "Mom?" I call hopefully.

"In here, Dov," Mom answers faintly from the living room, where I can hear the sounds of cable news. Sure enough, Mom's there with her chair pulled up right in front of the television screen. She's taken to doing this lately; I have a sneaking suspicion that she thinks if she sits close enough, eventually she might catch a glimpse of Brian. Still, if there's an opportunity to catch sight of Brian, Mom isn't going to miss it.

"I finished the lawn," I tell her.

"Mm-hm," she agrees distractedly, her eyes on the TV. *Wow, that's great, Dov. You've sure stepped up while your brother's been gone. Your father and I are so proud of you.*

"Dinner smells good."

"They're having a special report from Kabul," Mom murmurs, as if she hasn't heard me. She lifts a fingernail to her mouth and begins to gnaw at it. "There's been an attack on the consulate. I hope Brian wasn't involved; you don't think he was guarding it, do you, Dov? Or what if his unit was called to respond to the attack?"

I don't know what to say. "I'm sure he's fine," I murmur, then add, "The spaghetti's boiling. Do you want me to turn the burner down?"

"What?"

"The spaghetti? Should I take it off the stove?"

Finally she looks at me. "Oh, right. Yeah, could you turn it off? And just go ahead and eat, Dov; I'll have some later."

"Sure."

The spaghetti is good; I eat it alone at the kitchen table. Halfway through my second plateful, Sheba stalks into the room. I dip my finger into the sauce on my plate and hold my hand down to her level. "C'mere, crabby kitty," I say. Sheba regards me suspiciously, but the sight of what

I'm offering is more than she can resist. Warily, she sidles toward me in a sideways fashion, her nose twitching at the delicious smells in the air. When she's close enough, I lower my hand so she can lick the sauce from my finger, purring as she does it. It's a rare moment of détente between us.

"Now see?" I tell her after the sauce is gone and she's sniffing my hand to see if she's missed any. "I'm not so bad after all."

After I put my dishes in the dishwasher, I head to my room to feed Leo, who's watching for me from his aquarium. "Sorry," I apologize. "Late dinner tonight." I pinch a couple of fresh crickets from the container and drop them into his enclosure; without so much as a *thank you*, Leo begins to creep in their direction. "Ingrate," I mutter. It seems that no one appreciates my efforts.

I send a text to Ali but he doesn't respond, so I settle in to read tonight's assignment from *The Outsiders* by S. E. Hinton. Normally I don't bother too much with homework, but the book is actually kind of interesting. The main character is a kid named Ponyboy, and there's something about him that I can relate to. I lie down on my bed to read, and wake up some time later with my phone buzzing beneath my cheek.

"H'llo?" I mumble, half sleep-drunk.

"Hey." It's Miranda. "What are you doing?"

"Nothing. You?"

She yawns loudly into the phone. "Nothing. Bored."

"Yeah. Same here."

We sit in the dark in companionable silence. "Did your mom get her car fixed?" she asks.

Miranda and I have Twohey's class together, and afterwards I'd quickly filled her in on the reason for my summons to the office. "Yeah, it was no big deal. But when we got home, there was a message from Brian. We must have just missed him."

"Bet that bummed you out."

"Yeah, it kind of did. Nothing compared to what it did to my mom, though. I wish she'd gotten to talk to him. She's pretty much a 24/7 basket case."

"I thought people stationed overseas in the military could Skype with their families now."

I nod. "Supposedly they can, but for some reason our computer never works right when we try. Mom's had someone out to look at it twice."

"Bummer."

"Yeah." Suddenly I think of something. "Hey, did you guys find out anything more about that Scarlett chick after I left today?"

"Not really. As soon as you left, she came up with some random thing about having to make a phone call and took off. Just left her tray sitting there. Pretty lame if you ask me."

"Huh."

"Anyway," Miranda continues, "I'm going to bed, so I guess I'll talk to you tomorrow."

"'kay."

"G'night."

"'Night, Miranda."

I wonder what it is about talking to people that makes Scarlett so uneasy she's compelled to bolt. *I kind of do better on my own*, was what she told me; what, does the new girl have some kind of social phobia?

I can't say why I care, exactly, but something about the look in Scarlett's eyes when she said it makes me determined to find out.

SEVEN

(Fox News)—*The U.S. Military reports two U.S. helicopters crashed Monday in northern Afghanistan, killing six American troops. The crash happened around 3:15 a.m. local time. Afghan officials, speaking on condition of anonymity, said the crash site was in eastern Afghanistan near Khost, a city about 150 kilometers south of Kabul. According to an Associated Press count, the deaths raise to 3,561 the number of U.S. service members who have died in Operation Enduring Freedom since it began in October of 2001.*

....

Despite everything, I sleep hard that night, awakening only to the sound of my blaring alarm. "Holy crap," I croak, groping blindly for the off button.

I let myself wake up for a minute, then sit up, blinking. I'd read until I fell asleep; someone turned off my light and put *The Outsiders* facedown on my bedside table, open to the page where I'd left off. *Mom*, I think. Not many other possibilities.

In the bathroom, I see a man about a horse and splash some water on my face. I fell asleep in my clothes, so I decide to skip a shower and instead change into the argyle sweater I found on the vintage rack at the Salvation Army. It's perfectly shrunken and fits me like a glove, especially over a black T-shirt. I pull on jeans and loop my belt with the grommets through the belt loops, grab my things, and prepare to head out.

On my way through the kitchen, I grab a Coke out of the refrigerator and am nearly to the front door when I realize Mom is curled up on the sofa with a box of Kleenex. "Are you sick?" I ask. "Why aren't you at work?"

As the words come out of my mouth, I realize that Mom doesn't look ill; instead, her face is tracked with the shiny trails of tears I've seen too often lately. *Uh-oh*, I think. Living with Mom these days is like riding a roller coaster I can't get off. I glance at the clock, trying to be patient but not wanting to be late again.

"Oh, Dov," she quavers, shaking her head in despair, "I hardly slept at all last night. I was thinking about that story on the news last night … about the consulate or embassy or whatever it was. You don't think Brian's unit was there, do you? They said there were *casualties*, Dov. I'm just so afraid that Brian might be hurt, or that he might be … might even be … " She trails off, unable to say the words.

I let my backpack slide to the floor and make myself walk over to sit down next to her on the sofa. Setting my Coke on the floor, I pat her knee awkwardly. "Brian's fine, Mom," I tell her. "He sounded great when he called, remember?"

Mom nods, but then her face crumbles. "Oh, God," she wails, sobbing as if I just told her that I had it on good authority that Brian was reduced to a smoking pile of rubble. Watching too much war coverage on CNN has done this to her before, but she usually doesn't get quite *this* hysterical. I start feeling nervous; maybe Mom is finally losing it. "Mom…*Mom*," I say, trying to get her to listen to me. I wonder whether I should slap her or something, like in the movies. In the back of my mind is the worry that I really need to get going or I'm going to be late for first period again; after yesterday, I doubt Mertz will cut me any more breaks.

I summon Brian into my mind; I've found that in crisis situations, it sometimes helps to imagine what he would do in my shoes. Brian takes Mom by the shoulders, forcing her to look at me. "Listen," I order, my voice strong and calm. "*Brian. Is. Fine.* They would have called us if anything happened to him. No one called, so he's fine."

Mom sags between my hands, her blue eyes, so much like my brother's eyes, searching mine. "They would have called," she echoes. "They would have called. Yes, you're right, Dov…they would have called."

"You're just worn out, Mom. You need to get some sleep. Brian is fine. He'll call us as soon as he can. Brian is fine. He's fine." I repeat it calmly, like a mantra, until I see Mom's face relax and I know it's okay to loosen my grip on her. "You shouldn't even watch the news coverage," I scold, gently rubbing the spots where my fingers dug in to her arms. "It makes you too upset."

Mom nods. She reaches for a fresh Kleenex and draws a long, shuddering breath. "You're probably right," she sighs.

I wait a beat longer, until I'm sure the storm has passed and clearer sky is on the horizon. "Listen," I say in my Brian voice, "I've got to get to school, but I want you to go back to bed, okay?"

"Okay," Mom agrees meekly. "Back to bed."

"I'll call at lunchtime and check to see you're okay." I grab up my Coke and my backpack and am nearly to the door when she calls after me.

"Dov?"

"Yeah?" I hold my breath, hoping she isn't going to start up again.

Mom sniffles. "I don't want to hurt your feelings," she says, "but that sweater... my God... maybe you could... "

I pull the door shut between us, cutting off her voice.

The air outside is much colder than it was yesterday, and I wind up wishing I'd worn a jacket. The Gator's defrost takes a while to kick in, so by the time I've gone a few blocks toward school the windshield has begun to fog over from the inside. I have no choice but to roll down the window and stick my head out to see where I'm going.

With my head outside like that, it's hard to miss Scarlett standing on a corner, her arms wrapped around herself to try and keep warm as she waits for the bus. Her warm breath plumes out into the cold morning air, and I can see she's shivering even though she has a jacket on. The next thing I know, the Gator is pulling up to the curb in front of her.

Scarlett's first reaction is to scowl at whoever is blocking the bus stop, but when she realizes it's me, she quickly pulls open the Gator's passenger door and throws her backpack across the seat. "Thank *God*," she gasps, scooting in after it. "It's cold as hell out there."

"Probably not that much warmer in here," I apologize. "But better than standing outside."

Scarlett rubs her hands together in the flow of luke-warm air issuing weakly forth from the nearest heat vent.

"This is nothing," I tell her nonchalantly. The ability to weather the frigid temperatures of Minnesota is a source of pride for those of us who live here. "Doesn't it get cold where you come from?"

"Not this time of year," Scarlett says. "Why in the world do you have your window open?"

The defrost is finally catching up and the windshield is clearing. "I like the fresh air." I shrug. "But if it's too chilly for you, I can roll it up."

Scarlett raises an eyebrow at me. "Thanks," she says, half smiling. I suddenly remember her bottom lip, and I blush.

We ride a couple blocks without saying much. "So," Scarlett says suddenly, "what was that all about yesterday? When you got called to the office, I mean. You seemed kind of freaked out."

"It turned out to be nothing," I answer honestly. "I wasn't really freaked out, I just… I just didn't expect it." As well as Miranda asking, both Koby and Ali texted me after lunch to make sure everything was okay. I want to be friendly with Scarlett, but at this point I'm not sure we'll ever be friends, and until we are, I don't feel inclined to fill her in on the personal details of my life.

Scarlett doesn't press for more information, and I don't offer any. We make small talk the rest of the way to school, where I spot a surprisingly good parking space in the front of the lot. "Score!" I say, pointing to it.

"Winning," Scarlett agrees.

I pull into the spot, thinking that being patient with Mom has possibly brought me some good karma after all. Shutting off the Gator's ignition, I pocket the key and prepare to make the cold dash into school with time to spare when Scarlett speaks up.

"Look," she says, "there's something I wanted to tell you."

I sit back against the seat, surprised. "Yeah?"

"It's just … I'm kind of … you know, *sorry*. About yesterday. You were trying to be nice to me, and I wasn't very … "

"Nice?" I supply helpfully. "Cordial? The slightest bit pleasant?"

Scarlett smiles in spite of herself.

"Warm and sociable? Charming? Cheerful … "

"*All right*, Thesaurus Man," she says. "I get it. I could have been a little friendlier."

"A little?"

"Okay. A lot. I'm just … I'm dealing with some kind of intense stuff right now, Dov. Stuff with, uh, my family."

I laugh, more bitterly than I intended. "Hey," I say with a shrug, "join the club."

Scarlett tilts her head, regarding me. "You're right. It's not an excuse. I'm sorry and I appreciate the ride." She reaches for the door handle, about to get out of the car.

"Look," I say, "I'm just saying... *I get it*. Don't worry about it."

Scarlett nods. "Thanks."

An awkward pause later, we both climb out of the Gator and run for the school, gasping at the cold air.

"By the way," she huffs, glancing sideways at me, "nice sweater."

I lift my chin in acknowledgment. "Thanks."

Maybe there's hope for Scarlett after all.

EIGHT

....

Later that day, I'm hanging on the Commons, waiting for the bell to ring for Twohey's class. Koby is preparing to do his rabid chipmunk impression for Miranda, a routine that primarily involves lacing his teeth with White Blast toothpaste. Somehow he always manages to have a miniature tube of the stuff handy whenever the occasion calls for it. Miranda is already giggling in anticipation; the Rabid Chipmunk never gets old for her. I, on the other hand, have seen Koby's act too many times, and I'm kind of over it.

"Aaarghuhuhuhuh," Koby gargles, bucktoothed over foaming toothpaste. Above it all, his eyes roll and bulge crazily.

"Hahahaha," Miranda laughs, nearly falling over onto the table.

Across the Commons, I can see into the main office,

where Mr. Kerr is talking to Scarlett. She's listening intently, her eyes focused on the floor, until suddenly she spins and begins walking quickly away. Seeming determined to finish whatever he was saying, Kerr follows her out onto the Commons. Even from a distance, I can see Scarlett's face is red and she looks upset. Finally Kerr gives up and lets her go, but as he watches her walk away, I see his shoulders lift and then fall in a frustrated sigh. With a slight shake of his head, he turns and goes back into the office.

"What's with the drama queen?" Miranda asks. I turn to see that I haven't been the only one watching Scarlett storm away from the school counselor.

"Yeah," says Koby, sponging toothpaste foam off his T-shirt with a napkin. "Pretty intense."

"Who knows." I shrug. "I guess there's something going on with her family. We all know what that's like."

Both Koby and Miranda are silent, and I hope it means that they might view Scarlett with a little more compassion.

I stand up and grab my books off the table. "Maybe I'll go see if she's okay," I say, ignoring the looks exchanged by my friends.

"Later, man," Koby agrees, and Miranda shrugs.

I start off in the direction Scarlett disappeared a few minutes earlier. The kids who don't have first lunch are still in class, and most of the rest are on the Commons, so the halls are pretty empty. She isn't down the first hallway, or the second; I feel certain I'll find her in the library, but a quick scan reveals no evidence of Scarlett's two-tone hairdo there either. I'm just about to give up when I catch the sound of her voice coming from the direction of the art wing. *Perfect*; that's where I need to be for Twohey's class anyway. At the last minute, I slow my pace to an amble, not wanting Scarlett to think I'm stalking her.

I needn't have worried; she doesn't even see me coming around the corner. She's leaning against the wall, her back to me as she speaks indignantly into her cell phone. "But Mom," she's saying, "that's not fair. Why am I the one who has to stay away?" She listens for a minute. "Yeah, I mean, I get that. I just…" Her voice breaks. "Does Dad blame me? Please, just tell me if he does." She listens some more, her shoulders sagging at whatever the answer is. "I know," she says finally. "I said *I get it*. Okay. Yeah. Love you too. Tell Luke I miss him. Bye."

She snaps her phone closed. For a minute she doesn't move other than to lift a hand to wipe at her face with the cuff of her sweatshirt. When she turns and sees me standing there, her face registers first surprise, then embarrassment, and finally anger. "Eavesdrop much?!" she demands shrilly.

"Uh … n-no," I stammer, although in a way she's right. "I'm sorry. I mean, I wasn't trying to listen. I was just on my way to class…" I gesture toward the art room. "And you were there, and…"

"So you thought you'd listen in?" she accuses angrily, her gray eyes flashing like lightning. "Maybe pick up a little dirt on the new kid so you and your friends can have something to gossip about?"

"Don't be ridiculous, Scarlett, that's not what I was doing."

"Whatever." Still furious, she tries to storm past me but I surprise us both by grabbing her arm.

"Look," I tell her, "what makes you think you're the only one whose life sucks?"

Scarlett's eyes narrow. "Oh really?" she spits. "You've got problems too? Gee, Dov, I'm sorry you don't have the *funds* to fill your gas tank," she coos sarcastically. "I'm sorry you're having a bad *hair* day. Your life is really tragic, I'm sure."

She tears her arm away from me and for a moment I'm so stunned by the fury of her words that I can't move or think of anything nasty enough in response. I stare into her challenging face, and suddenly something in her eyes makes me stop trying to find the right words to burn her back. Instead, I take a deep breath. "Look," I say evenly, "I get it. We *all* get it. You don't want friends, you don't *need* friends, and that's fine." Overhead, the bell rings for next period, and in an instant the hallway is teeming with kids. "I'm sorry I pretended to care."

I let myself be swept into the current swirling in the direction of Twohey's class. "And for your information," I call back, "I think I'm having a pretty *good* hair day."

I turn my back on Scarlett just as it hits me what I saw deep in her eyes; not anger, but something more familiar. Something that looks an awful lot like pain.

STAY TUNED AFTER THESE MESSAGES
FOR ANOTHER EXCITING EPISODE OF
THE DOV HOWARD FAIL SHOW!

NINE

....

For the next hour, I try to put the incident with Scarlett out of my mind and focus all my attention on the chalk drawing I'm working on. I'm so into it I barely even notice when Ms. Twohey bends in close for a look at my progress. "Interesting, Dov," she says. "Give me some idea of what's inspiring you here. Do you have a muse?"

I set down my chalk and try to see my piece the way Ms. Twohey sees it. It takes a minute for me to realize that the changes I've made to my goth version of Alice in Wonderland make her look awfully familiar. A lot like Scarlett, in fact.

"Uh, not really," I tell her, hurriedly erasing a few lines with the side of my hand. Being in such close proximity to Ms. Twohey usually makes my hands start to shake and renders me unable to produce any of the witty-beyond-my-years remarks that spring to mind so easily when I'm lying in bed at night imagining this kind of situation.

"Where do you see this piece going from here?" she prompts.

"I don't know," I sigh. "I'm kind of distracted today, actually. Maybe I should just start over."

Ms. Twohey straightens up and gives me one of her dazzling smiles; the kind that's usually guaranteed to keep my heart thumping irregularly for the rest of class. "No," she says, "it's unexpected. Keep working on it."

She moves on down the aisle, trailing behind her the scent of expensive perfume.

I lay my chalk down in the tray and indulge myself in a full fifteen seconds of watching her lovingly.

Teen Challenges Supreme Court, Citing "Freedom to Love."

(AP) Sixteen-year-old Dov Howard of Longview, Minn., has taken his bid to be allowed to marry his art teacher, Ms. Denise Twohey, all the way to the country's highest court, reports the Minnesota Free Press. "I have to say, I stand behind Mr. Howard on this one," commented Justice Antonin Scalia. "Where does the constitution suggest we should stand in the way of destiny? When two people are meant to be together, we as a country should celebrate it, not ..."

Your life is really tragic, I'm sure. Scarlett's sneering words interrupt my Twohey-focused reverie.

I shake her voice out of my head and crane my neck to

look. Miranda is two easels over, staring gloomily at her canvas with her chin in her hand. "Hey," I call softly. "Miranda!"

She lifts her head and turns to look at me; her chin is smudged with dark chalk, making her look like she's sprouted a five o'clock shadow. "Hey, Dov." She smiles.

"How's the angel coming?"

Miranda sighs wearily. "It's not." She gets up and comes over to stand behind me so she can look at what I'm working on. Sheepish, I fight the urge to cover up my drawing; if Miranda sees any traces of Scarlett in what I've drawn, I'll never hear the end of it.

She says nothing for a minute, then finally, "Huh."

"Ms. Twohey thinks it's 'interesting.' And by 'interesting,' I'm pretty sure she means 'brilliant.'" The art world is a competitive place.

Miranda picks up a piece of chalk from my tray and reaches over me. A few well-placed strokes later and my Alice looks much improved.

"Wow," I say, impressed.

Miranda hands me the chalk. "Sometimes you just need another eye."

"Or another artist."

Miranda laughs, then dusts her hands back and forth against each other, sending chalk motes floating into the air. "So," she says, "did you track down the Scarlett Letter?"

I nod. "She wasn't in the mood to talk."

"Big surprise there." Miranda crosses her arms. "So, you like that chick?"

"She's okay."

"You planning to hook up with her?"

"What? Don't be retarded." Even as I say it, I wonder whether Miranda is right. There's no denying Scarlett is an attractive girl, and no denying I feel attracted to her. Guiltily, I glance at Ms. Twohey, who's helping Arden Barry improve his shading.

"Dov." Miranda smiles patiently. "You're *never going to get Ms. Twohey.*"

I go back to working on Alice's hair. "You never know."

"No, I think we both ... " Miranda trails off. I wait for her to finish, but she doesn't.

"Dov," she says faintly instead, and her tone makes me look up quickly. With a lift of her chin, Miranda indicates something happening behind me, across the room. I turn, and see Mr. Kerr standing in the door of the art room. His face is serious and he's looking at me; when he lifts a hand and beckons, I know everything has changed.

Out in the hall, Kerr starts to apologize for pulling me out of class, but I cut him off. "Just tell me," I demand. "It's Brian, isn't it? Something happened to my brother."

Kerr nods. "I don't really know any details. Your mom called and she was pretty upset. I thought it was best for you to go home as quickly as possible. Are you ... would you like me to drive you?"

Something weird seems to be happening to the sights and sounds around me. Kerr's voice is muffled and hard to hear, but when my head swivels toward the parking lot where the Gator waits, I actually hear the sound of my neck creak. None of the colors in the hallway seem right; I feel like Alice at her tea party where nothing is as it should be.

An odd buzzing has sprung up in my head, making it hard to think. Mr. Kerr nods, and his lips are moving but the only words that break the surface are "an incident." *An incident;* I can only imagine what those words have done to Mom ...

"I've got to go home," I say.

"Yes, of course," Kerr agrees. He takes a half step toward me as if he's about to pull me into a hug, but I spin around him, out of reach. If Mr. Kerr, or anyone else, hugs me I'll lose it, and that's not something I can risk right now.

The next thing I know I'm outside, running through the cold air toward the Gator. My chest is burning and the rest of my body is numb, but in my mind, only one thought echoes.

Brian.

TEN

....

We all gather in the living room to stare at the television and each other while waiting for the next call. Dad stews grimly in the recliner while Mom and Victoria huddle together on the sofa, murmuring words of comfort to each other. They've worked their way through a full box of Kleenex each. I sit on the floor, my back against the wall. *Survivor* is on, but none of us are following the action.

Shortly after seven p.m., when the phone finally rings in the kitchen, everyone in the room stiffens. Mom covers her mouth with one hand and with the other reaches out to grasp Victoria's. I watch as new tears fill her eyes.

Dad takes a deep breath. "I'll answer it," he says, getting up and hurrying into the kitchen. Back in the living room, I draw my knees up so I can rest my chin on them, my arms wrapping themselves around my legs. It feels better to listen this way, my body folded up in defense against whatever I'm about to hear.

"This is Michael Howard," I hear Dad say grimly, then silence. I feel my own heart pounding in my chest; whatever is being said to Dad is going to affect every one of us for the rest of our lives.

"I see," Dad says, his voice breaking. "Yes, I understand. We're just so relieved to hear that he's alive."

Victoria lets out a whoop. "He's alive!" she cries. "He's okay!"

Mom breaks into fresh, happy sobs as she and Victoria hug and laugh and cry. I let out the breath I didn't realize I was holding and rake my hands through my hair, unable to hold back the silly grin that's taken over my face. Brian is alive. *Brian is alive.* It doesn't matter whether he's jacked up or not, as long as I know I'll get to see my brother again.

In the kitchen, Dad's still on the phone. "Uh-huh, ... yep ... " he's saying. "Hold on a minute, let me get a pen." I can hear him walking in circles, searching. Because he's gone so much, sometimes Dad forgets where we keep things.

I get to my feet and go into the kitchen where Dad is still circling aimlessly. Retrieving a pen and notepad from the drawer next to the refrigerator, I hand them over.

"Yessir, I'm ready," he says into the phone. Silence, then Dad jotting a few things down. "So, do you think we'll hear something more soon?" He listens, as the person on the other end commits to whatever he can. "Okay," Dad says. "Well, that's wonderful ... wonderful news. Thank you, sir. Thank you for calling." I can honestly say I've never heard

Dad call anyone "sir" before; his terminology is usually more colorful and less respectful.

Dad hangs up the phone, then stands motionless for a moment, his hand still on the receiver. "Jesus Christ, thank God," I hear him mutter.

"Mick?" Mom's in the kitchen doorway, her tearstained face hopeful. Victoria peers from behind her with wide eyes. "What did you find out?"

"He's hurt, but he's alive, Laura. We can be thankful for that. They're still trying to figure out exactly what happened."

Fractures ... the officer had told Dad ... *facial trauma* ... *a concussion.* There'd been some kind of explosion while Brian's unit was out on patrol. Despite being seriously injured, Brian had survived, but four other soldiers in his unit were killed.

"Their poor families!" Mom cries, horrified. "I feel terrible that we've gotten this good news while they're all hearing that ... that ... " She turns away and walks back into the living room, slowly, like she's suddenly become a hundred years old.

I thought she'd go after Mom, but Victoria comes further into the kitchen. "Where is he?" she demands. "Where's Brian at now?"

"Germany," Dad says. "They flew him there to stabilize him. Once he's well enough to make the trip, he'll be coming home."

"Coming home?!" Victoria cries. She turns and grabs me by the shoulders, then throws her arms around my neck. "He's coming home! Brian's coming home!"

"Yeah," I agree. "That's awesome. Obviously."

"You're damn right it is," Dad says. He heads into the living room where Mom is standing by the window, staring blankly out into the darkness. I watch as Dad draws her to him, wrapping her in his arms until Mom relaxes and leans back into him. I can't remember the last time I witnessed such a display of affection between my parents; if, in fact, I *ever* have.

"Brian's coming ho-ome! Brian's coming ho-ome!" Victoria's dancing around the kitchen, singing the words.

I can't help but smile. *Brian's coming home!* It's all I can do not to sing the words right along with her.

ELEVEN

(Reuters)—*A suicide bombing that took place near the German embassy in Kabul killed no U.S. troops, although there were several civilian casualties reported…*

....

This morning, I'm thinking about Brian even before I've opened my eyes. When I try to picture what might have happened to him, I start to get a sick feeling in my stomach so I push the whole thing out of my mind and sit up. The truth is, I *can't* imagine what it's like to be in his military-issue combat boots, to watch people being killed—and maybe killing people himself—all the while fearing for his own life. I wonder whether Brian will be different when he returns, or if he's still the person who flashed me a peace sign from the steps of the plane before he left. Then again, how can anyone who's experienced military conflict *not* be permanently changed?

I stretch my arms up over my head; being that it's

Saturday, there's nowhere I have to be. Under my pillow, my cell phone vibrates.

"Hello?" I answer, stifling a still-waking-up yawn.

"Hi... Dov?"

I don't answer. If my ears aren't deceiving me, on the other end of the line is the last person I expect to hear from.

"It's Scarlett."

"Yeah, I know."

"If you're wondering, I got your number from Koby. He told me about your brother over in Afghanistan, and that something awful had happened. I'm really sorry, Dov."

"We got a call last night," I tell her. "He's hurt pretty bad, but he's probably going to be okay."

Through the phone, Scarlett breathes a sigh. "That's awesome," she says, and the relief in her voice sounds genuine. "I really mean it."

"Yeah. Thanks. We were pretty relieved too."

"Listen, Dov, I was wondering... do you want to maybe hang out for a little while today? I wanted to talk to you about something."

Scarlett sounds nervous, but I can't resist. "About how my pathetic little problems aren't important compared to yours?"

The other end of the line is quiet for so long I start to wonder whether she's hung up on me. I try not to care, but I feel a little bad. "Look," she says finally. "Just give me a chance to explain. I promise I won't bite your head off like that again."

I consider. "All right. Meet me at the Red Pepper. Two o'clock."

"Okay," she says immediately.

I hang up without asking if she knows how to get there, or even saying goodbye.

Leo is tough to track down in his aquarium; I finally locate him lying under the foliage beside his cave. It isn't his usual spot to hang out. "Tired this morning?" I ask, fishing around with one hand in the cricket motel.

Tired of this program.

"You and me both," I agree. I captured a fat cricket and dangle it temptingly by one leg in front of Leo's nose. "Winner, winner, chicken dinner!" I prompt.

To my surprise, Leo turns his pointy nose away, letting his eyes drift closed. "Huh," I say. Usually Leo is more than ready to chase down his breakfast. "All right then." I shrug and drop the cricket onto the aquarium floor. It scrambles for cover and disappears. "Save it for brunch."

Thinking that a little music might stimulate Leo's appetite, I slide the Violent Femmes album out of its sleeve and place it carefully on the record-playing platform. The needle lands gently in the first groove, and a moment later the pure, urgent strains of "Blister in the Sun" are floating through the air. I'm in a weekend mood, so I sing along, straining to match Gordon Gano's falsetto.

"Jesus Christ, Dov." Dad is at my door, his face unshaven and his expression irritated. "Do you have to play that crap right now? Your mother's asleep; she had a helluva day yesterday, and I think she could use the rest."

"Oh," I say, startled. "Sorry." Quickly I reach across to turn the volume down. When Dad continues to glare at me, I change my mind and press the power button to turn the player off entirely.

Dad turns to leave, then changes his mind and turns back. "Clean up this pigsty before you go anywhere. And don't even get me started about that hair. Your brother will be here soon and he's coming home with a Purple Heart. The least that you can do is to show some respect around here."

I concentrate on fitting the album back into its sleeve; when I look up again, Dad is gone.

Across the room, Leo has decided to wake up after all and is watching me from his aquarium, an inscrutable expression on his pointy face. "Life's a bitch and then you die," I inform him.

Unless you're Brian Howard, in which case you're only seriously wounded, Leo reminds me.

With a sigh, I toss the Femmes album on top of the others, then think better of it and gather them all into an untidy stack. I kick dirty clothes into my closet and pull the bedspread up over tangled blankets. It's unlikely that Dad will check back, but there's no point taking chances. He doesn't need any more reason to resent me beyond the fact that it's Brian, not me, who's had to narrowly escape a terrible and untimely death.

Things Not to Get Dad for Christmas
DVD of Sophie's Choice
Framed copy of my birth certificate or report card
Frommer's Top Ten U.S. Boarding Schools

TWELVE

....

The Red Pepper is always busy on Saturdays, but when I don't spot Scarlett at any of the crowded tables I start to wonder if she's stood me up. If she has, well ... I'm used to a certain amount of disrespect, but this is ridiculous.

"Hey, Howard!" The brain-piercing screech of Ray Sellers' voice cuts through the noise of the sandwich shop. Sure enough, there he is, sitting with a few of his cronies at a table near the side door. "What're you doing here?" he calls. "I didn't think kids like you ate!"

I spot Scarlett in a booth farther toward the back of the place. "Twice in one week," I observe as I pass. "How did I get so lucky?"

Ray grins. "Better run home and write a sad poem about it," he calls after me, causing his table to break into laughter.

Scarlett has changed her hair color; it's darker, and

instead of the red fringes, a streak of purple runs through her bangs. Though I'm still pissed at her, I can't help but notice how pretty she is. *So, do you want to hook up with her?* Miranda asked. Remembering it almost makes me angrier.

"Hi, Dov," she says humbly as I approach.

"Hey," I say, shrugging as I slide into the booth. "How's it going?"

"All right, I guess." Up close, her eyes are red-rimmed; I can't tell if it's makeup or if she's been crying. If Ray sees her, he'll probably bring out his entire library of "crying emo kids" jokes. However I feel about Scarlett these days, it's pretty clear that whatever is going on in her life is no laughing matter.

I pick up a menu and pretend to read it, even though I always have the same thing at the Pepper: three Schneiders and a cheese tostada. "Did you order?" I ask Scarlett.

"No," she replies. "I thought I'd see what you were having. And just so you know, since I asked you here, I'm paying."

"Fine with me."

A minute later the waitress comes over. She takes in our hair and clothes, but to her credit doesn't make the kind of expression adults usually make when they're faced with us. "What can I get you two?" she asks.

I give her our order and the waitress departs. I watch Scarlett's hands twist together on the table between us and stubbornly let the silence go on. I don't feel like I owe Scarlett anything at this point.

"So," she says finally. "I guess I owe you another apology. It's getting pretty old, huh?"

I don't respond.

"Look, Dov," Scarlett sighs. "First of all, I'm sorry I made it sound like your problems weren't anything. I felt so bad after Koby filled me in on the situation with your brother. Koby made him sound like some kind of super-human."

I nodded. "I'm not half as good at even *one* thing as Brian is at pretty much everything." That pretty much sums it up, I figure.

"Some people are like that," Scarlett agrees. "Everything they do always works out, like, perfectly. It must be amazing."

"Yeah. This is like the first bad thing that's ever happened to him."

"Almost getting killed?"

"I mean being deployed. Sent to Afghanistan," I say. "And then to actually be coming back like … however he's going to come back." The "however" part remains to be seen.

"Anyway," I add, "just the fact that he's coming home at all will make things at my house a thousand times better. Up until now, my mom's been pretty much freaking out 24/7."

The waitress returns with our drinks, and I watch Scarlett strip the paper off her straw, her lips pressed together into a tight line. "I'm sure he'll be glad to be back too," she says grimly. "It really sucks being away from the people you care about."

The tension between us lessens and we make small talk for a while, mostly about school. I want to ask Scarlett about *her* family problems, but something tells me that if I do, she'll go skittering away like a frightened deer. If she wants to tell me her situation, it will have to be on her terms.

"Here you go," the waitress says when she finally sets paper plates heaping with food down in front of us. Eating at the Red Pepper is a no-frills experience, but the food is cheap and delicious.

"Those are Schneiders," I tell Scarlett, indicating the pile of tacos in front of her. "A Pepper specialty."

Scarlett takes a bite. "Whoa," she says through her first mouthful.

"Spicy, I know... it's the secret sauce. But good, right?"

She nods and takes a long pull on her Coke. "Really good," she agrees.

We chow down, and it isn't long before there's nothing in front of us but empty paper plates dotted with stray bits of lettuce and random smears of sauce. I see Scarlett stifle a belch, so I let a mighty one rumble out. "Incoming," I apologize.

To her credit, Scarlett laughs, and I do too. When we get over it, Scarlett looks at me thoughtfully. "Listen," she says, "if I tell you some stuff, can it just be, you know, between us?"

I shrug. "Yeah," I say. "Sure."

Scarlett leans forward, her face serious. "No, I really mean it, Dov. I know I don't know you a whole lot yet, but I just feel like I have to talk to someone besides..."

"Mr. Kerr?"

She smiles. "I mean, nothing against the guy... he's nice and all, but..."

"No, I get it," I tell her. "Don't worry. Whatever you have to say, it's in the vault."

Scarlett takes a sip of her Coke. "The thing is," she says, "I kind of got sent here to Longview. It's not like … I mean, I didn't want to come."

"Did you get in some kind of trouble or something?"

She laughs in a way that's pretty much the opposite of laughing. "I guess that's one way of looking at it. Look, you have to promise that you won't judge me."

"My family is the Dysfunctionals. I'm in no position to judge."

Scarlett nods, then takes a deep breath. "And that it will stay just between us."

I give her a look that says, *haven't we been over this before?*

"Yeah, well, that's what Kerr says too," Scarlett points out. "But I think he talks to my mom. So anyway," she continues, "my dad and my uncle James … his stepbrother … they grew up really close, like real brothers. My dad's the older one, and from what my mom says, he was kind of a surrogate father to James."

"Uh-huh."

"James has always been kind of a drinker, which caused problems when he'd show up bombed for holiday dinners. Dad would make excuses for him, and then Mom would call him and Grandma 'enablers' because they put up with it."

"Huh." We've studied this sort of thing in Psychology—alcoholics, enabling, and family members with co-dependency—but I've never heard a real-life account of it from someone I know.

"Last spring," Scarlett continues, "my uncle lost his job and his apartment, so of course Dad told him he could move in with us."

"Why didn't he move in with your grandma?" I ask.

"Grandma lives in an assisted living facility. She couldn't have him staggering around the place, falling into the potted plants."

"Yeah."

"Mom was furious, of course, and threatened to leave; they argued and argued about it. 'He's my only brother,' my dad said. 'I can't just let him live at the Mission like a bum.' 'You have to face facts,' Mom said. 'Your brother *is* a bum.' I think she felt bad that she said it, though, because a little bit after that she said he could stay for a week or two. So my uncle came to live with us."

Having only one brother myself, I can kind of understand Scarlett's dad's position. I know that no matter how bad things might get for me or Brian, we'd never let the other one be homeless. "So, that's why they sent you away?" I guess. "Because your mom didn't want you around your uncle's drinking?"

Scarlett sighs. "No," she says. "I wish they'd sent me away right when he got there. Then maybe none of this would have happened." She pauses. "My uncle had been living with us for about three weeks when I came home from school one day and found him sitting in the living room, completely wasted. 'Hey, there,'" he called when he saw me come in. 'Come over here and give me a kiss.'"

"What?!"

Scarlett nods. "I told him to stop being a puke and went to my room. I thought about calling my mom, but I knew that he'd get kicked out for sure then, and so I was kind of debating what to do when all of the sudden I heard him coming down the hall, bumping into walls and stuff."

I chuckle involuntarily, but something tells me nothing about this story is funny.

"The next thing I know, he's standing in my doorway all unsteady, looking like he doesn't even know where he is. 'Get the hell out of here, James,' I told him, and for a minute I thought he was going to leave, but then he didn't, and I started to get kind of scared. Because I could tell he was so drunk he maybe didn't even know it was me, and I just didn't know what he was going to do."

Scarlett's eyes are on the table now. "So before I could even scream or anything, he was, like *on* me."

"Holy crap."

Scarlett's face is flushed, remembering. "It was disgusting," she shudders. "His hot breath right in my face, and *oh my God*, he smelled awful, but he was still so strong and he pushed me down on the bed and his hands were all over me, and I knew he was going to ... "

"Jesus."

"He wasn't in his right mind ... I'm not sure if he *ever* really was anymore ... and suddenly I realized that nobody was going to be home for a long time. No one was going to ... save me, you know. But just when I thought I was going to have to let it happen, something in my mind kind of snapped, and I just *freaked out*. I mean, I'd been fighting him off and all, but I just got, like, crazy and hysterical. That must have gotten through to him, because suddenly he just let me go. He got up, somehow, and staggered out of the room. I didn't even care where he went; all I could think of was getting to the shower so I could get his *reek* off of me."

"I'm sure."

Scarlett swallows. "When I came out of the shower, James was gone, which was fine by me. I locked the doors and called my mom. I told her James was drunk and had taken off and she'd better come home. She must have called my dad, because he got there first. When he opened the garage door to park the car, there he was."

I just stare at her, unable to imagine what horrible thing she's going to say next. "Your uncle?"

Scarlett nods, dry-eyed. "He'd hanged himself. I guess even Uncle James had a conscience, or else maybe he was just feeling sorry for himself, knowing he'd finally burned his last bridge."

"So I don't understand," I say after a moment. "Why did *you* get sent away?"

"Doesn't make much sense, does it? My dad was a terrible mess, which I get, of course. We had the funeral and buried the bastard, but my dad couldn't handle it all. He couldn't stop crying, and talking about poor James and how *depressed* he'd been and how nothing had ever worked out for James…"

"But what about *you*?" I ask. "Weren't they upset about what he'd tried to do to you?"

"They didn't really know about it."

"You didn't tell them?"

Scarlett sighs. "No. I knew it would only make things worse, and my dad was already such a mess."

I guess I can understand. Sometimes it's not worth rocking the boat when everyone's already seasick.

"But I kept having all these nightmares about it, and then I started to think I could *smell* him; that putrid smell just seemed to *live* in my nostrils. I started having panic attacks. I even did … this." She turns her wrists over so I can see the faint white lines etched in her skin.

"You cut?"

Scarlett nods. "I'm a cliché, right? But it was weird, Dov—something about it made me feel better, at least at first."

I don't know what to say.

"Anyway, my gym teacher saw the marks and called my parents. So I basically had no choice. I told them."

"How did it go?" I ask.

"Not great, obviously. Mom started freaking out and crying. Dad looked … well, I don't even like to think about it. All these years, he'd stood up for his loser brother, and in the end, Uncle James hurts the person my dad cares about the most in the world."

"Yeah."

"Finally, I guess, Dad just couldn't take it anymore, so he took off. A few hours later we got a call from the cops—he'd picked a fight in a bar and was in the hospital with a fractured skull and bleeding on the brain. They weren't sure he'd live, but he did. Once he was medically stable, they transferred him to the psychiatry unit; Mom went up to visit him, but he didn't want to see me right away. He couldn't bear the guilt, he said. Couldn't even look at my face."

"That's understandable," I say.

"Is it?"

"I don't know," I admit. "Maybe."

"All I know," Scarlett says harshly, "is that in the end, everyone decided that it would be better for me to come here and stay with my grandparents until Dad can get things figured out. 'Your father's fragile right now,' Mom says. "He just needs some time.'"

"*He's* fragile?" I sputter. "What about you?"

Scarlett nods. "Right? I suppose they think they're helping me by having me see Mr. Kerr. They wanted me to see a regular psychiatrist... you know, like a medical doctor... but I put my foot down. The way this thing has played out, I'd find myself locked up in a psych unit on the wrong end of some shock therapy."

"Is it helping?" I ask. "Talking to Kerr?"

Scarlett considers. "I guess it must be," she says. "I mean, I don't dream about it anymore. And I've pretty much stopped feeling so pissed off all the time. Kerr has me keeping a journal. That helps too."

"I can see why you probably didn't want to talk about it."

"Yeah. It's just been a lot to sort out, and sometimes I feel like if the wrong thing happens, I'll just sort of... shatter."

"You're fragile too," I say.

Scarlett smiles ruefully. "Fragile," she says. "It's the new black."

Press Release

Vanguard Records announces the November 16th release of the new LP by ground-breaking punk lyricist D-Dog Howard and the Fragile Psyche Band. The much-anticipated album, "Broken Dreams and Shattered Spirit," is the band's first album since their freshman effort, 2010's "Pointless Days and Wasted Nights" and Howard's soulful chart-topping single, "Twohey, To Me." ...

THIRTEEN

....

"Can I get you two kids anything else?" The waitress is back, our ticket in her hand.

Scarlett shakes her head. "No," I tell her, "we're good."

"Okay, then." The waitress drops the ticket on the table, closer to me than to Scarlett.

Scarlett grins. "I'm going to the restroom," she tells me. "Don't pay that while I'm gone."

"Don't worry." I watch her go, still struggling to wrap my mind around everything she's told me.

"Dov?"

I'm so distracted by my thoughts that I actually jump when the familiar voice calls my name.

Miranda is waving to me from the counter near the Pepper's front door. "Hey!" I say, surprised and happy to see her.

Miranda scoots between tables until she arrives at ours.

I slide out of my seat and give her a quick, friendly hug, feeling her cold cheek press against mine "What's up?"

"My mom sent me to pick up lunch," Miranda tells me. I always feel a little awkward when Miranda calls her foster parents "mom" and "dad," but I guess a surrogate family is better than no family at all. "How about you?" she adds, surveying the remains of Scarlett's meal. "You here with Ali?"

"No…"

"Oh, Koby?"

I'm just opening my mouth to explain when Scarlett herself appears, coming back from the bathroom. "Hey, Miranda," she says, obviously surprised to see her.

The parts of Miranda's face that aren't already flushed from cold turned pink. "Oh," she says, looking at me oddly. "Hi, Scarlett. So you guys are, like, here together?"

"Yeah," I say. I know Miranda probably thinks it's pretty random for me to be here with Scarlett after I said I was done with her. "You should hang out with us while you wait for your food," I suggest.

Before Miranda can reply, Scarlett breaks in. "Listen," she says, "I've got to run, anyway. I just remembered I'm supposed to take my grandma to Costco. They've got toilet paper in bulk, you know."

I laugh, but I'm confused. Suddenly she has to leave?

Scarlett is digging in her purse. "Here," she says abruptly, shoving some money at me. "This should cover it."

"Wait…" I'm going to tell her I was only joking about letting her pay for the whole thing, but before I can finish she's grabbed her jacket and bolted out the door with not so much as a "see ya."

"Sheesh, was it something I said?" Miranda asks. Her face has gone back to its normal color.

"I don't know," I say. "I guess that's just Scarlett."

After I leave the Pepper, I decide to detour over to Ali's place instead of heading home. There's no question in my mind as to whether Ali will be around; he rarely goes anywhere. The Gabols live in a nice neighborhood, and I wonder whether they'll mind the Gator being parked on the street in front of their house. Nevertheless, I slide it up along the curb and park, then run up the lawn to the front door.

"Hello, Dov," Ali's dad greets me when he comes to the door. Dr. Gabol is the opposite of my dad; a pleasant, dark-skinned man who's actually interested in his son and his son's friends. He and Ali's mom, Dr. Saraphine Gabol, are accustomed to their son's eccentricities and unconventional fashion choices; as long as Ali has a few human-like friends and isn't posing a general threat to society, the Gabols seem content to sit back and watch the evolution of the unique specimen they've created.

"My son is in his room," Dr. Gabol tells me. "Most likely playing that online game he enjoys so much. *Darkworld*, I believe it's called."

"*Dark*scape," I correct, slipping off my Converses. The Gabols have a strict "no shoes in the house" policy.

Dr. Gabol nods. "I knew it was Dark something," he agrees.

Ali's completely obsessed with *Darkscape*, an online

virtual world where players reinvent themselves as characters of a medieval community. But *Darkscape* is Ali's thing, not mine; if I'm online, it's usually just to download music or watch videos on YouTube.

As predicted, I find Ali in his room. His hair is rumpled and he's wearing a T-shirt and pajama pants, suggesting that he simply awakened that morning, rolled out of bed, and landed in front of his computer.

"Hey," he says without looking up.

"Hey." I drop into a worn-out recliner near the window. "What's happening? Anything new with the red-head?"

On the screen beyond Ali, hundreds of characters are milling around, conducting their medieval business. For reasons known only to him, his alter-ego on *Darkscape* is a tall, auburn-haired female character named RedWarrior23.

Ali nods. "Actually," he says grimly, "I've gotten myself into something of a *situation.*"

"Really."

"You remember my stalker?"

I do; a while back, Ali mentioned that another of the online players, Moridin, kept popping up everywhere; at the jousting games, in the marketplace, in the forest. It had started to get creepy when Moridin began offering RedWarrior23 gifts; at last count, Ali had scored a pair of leather boots, a longbow, and several pies.

"What now," I ask. "More pie?"

"No," Ali mutters. "Ten thousand drachms." Drachms are the official currency of *Darkscape*, and even I know ten thousand drachms is a small fortune.

"Where'd he get that kind of scratch?"

"Won it in the tournaments, I guess," Ali says. "Turns out he's the Tiger Woods of the joust."

"Not necessarily a good thing."

"Seriously, no one can beat him." There's an unmistakable note of admiration in Ali's voice.

"Why would he give all that money to RedWarrior23?"

Ali throws me a grin. "Obviously, I'm irresistible."

"That's a little messed up, bro."

"If you think *that's* messed up, wait until you hear *this*," Ali says. "He wants me to marry him."

"*Marry* him?!" I choke. "Can you even *do* that?"

Ali shrugs. "He says he knows a cleric who can perform the ceremony."

I'm momentarily at a loss for words. Finally I find some. "You're not going to do it, are you?"

Ali shrugs. "I don't know. I mean, it's hard to say no to a thousand drachms. I could buy a horse, so I wouldn't have to walk everywhere anymore."

I couldn't believe that he was even considering it. "Ali," I remind him, "you'd be married to a *dude*."

"Only on the game, bro. No one else would have to know about it." He looks at me sternly. "Right?"

I'm somewhat relieved to know that even who-cares-what-people-think Ali considers this to be an issue worthy of discretion. "Well," I ask finally, "do ya even love the guy?"

Ali smiles. "Apparently, for the right price, even *my* love can be bought. And listen, Dov—if you sign up for a *Darkscape* account, you can be the damsel of honor."

"Funny."

Ali types in a few commands to log off. "You hungry?" he asks when the screen goes blank.

"Nah."

We head out to the kitchen, where Ali finds a mixing bowl and pours it full of Cocoa Krispies. "So," he says, inspecting a spoon he's pulled from the kitchen dish drainer. "Pretty good news about your brother, huh?"

I spoke to Ali last night, after we got the news about Brian. "Yeah. It was just good to hear that he's alive and out of danger. I'll bet my mom slept okay last night for the first time since he's been gone."

Ali is pouring milk over his cereal. "What happened anyway?"

"I guess there was some kind of explosion while his unit was out on patrol. Probably one of those roadside bombs, or whatever they call it … an IUD or something."

We head to the family room, where we sprawl on the Gabols' leather couches. Ali's family doesn't have a television, so there's no sound other than the slurping noises Ali makes inhaling his cereal. I'm grateful when piano music suddenly comes floating down the hall; besides being a biology professor, Ali's mom is also a concert pianist, so she practices a lot. Since Ali's dad plays the violin, there are times when being at Ali's house can feel like a visit to the symphony.

"We should call Koby and see if he wants to hang with us at the mall," Ali suggests when he's drained the last of the milk from his bowl. "Maybe catch a movie or something."

"Sure." I agree, reaching for my cell phone. "I'm supposed to get a haircut too ... my dad kind of flipped out about it this morning."

Ali nods; he knows all about my dad.

"The funny thing is," I add, "I don't think he even realized my hair was a different color. He just knew that there was *something* he didn't like about me."

"Nice."

I scroll down my contacts list for Koby's name. "Maybe we can check out the bridal stores," I tell Ali. "What are you, a size medium?"

WEDDING ANNOUNCEMENT

Darkscape's own Hero of the Joust, the renowned and wealthy Sir Moridin, has announced his betrothal to the statuesque and ginger-haired beauty known as RedWarrior23. Although the bride has been referred to by suspicious locals as "a gold digger" and "a bit off," the ceremony will be performed by the Honorable Vicar Baldor in the Merry Men Glen on October 25 at 5 p.m. All friends, relatives, dwarves, and elves are invited to attend. Given the groom's legendary reputation as a skilled assassin, no one is expected to object to the union.

FOURTEEN

··

We don't hear any more news about Brian for the rest of the weekend, and by Monday morning, Dad's decided that there's no reason why he shouldn't head back out on the road.

"You can call me if you hear anything," he tells Mom. She's gone from elation over Brian's being safe back to worry about exactly how badly he's been hurt.

"What if he takes a turn for the worse, Mick?" she demands. "What if I have to make some decision about his treatment?"

"I'm a cell phone call away, Laura," Dad tells her impatiently, packing his cooler full of sandwiches and fruit for the road. He has a fridge in the sleeper of his truck, and likes to save money and time by bringing some of his food along. "Grab me a carton of cigarettes out of the cupboard, will you?" he asks her.

My attempt to pass through the kitchen hidden behind a shield of invisibility fails. "So, I guess that's your half-assed idea of a haircut, huh?" Dad snaps at me.

I'm not surprised by his reaction, necessarily. My hair *is* shorter, there's no denying that, and there were definitely scissors involved. I should know; in the end, I decided to skip Cost-Cutters and take a whack at it myself. To my surprise, I was pretty happy with the effect .

Behind him, Mom purses her lips but doesn't say anything; I imagine she doesn't want to waste any of her anger at Dad on me.

I grab a banana for breakfast, deciding to take my breakfast on the run. "See ya," I say to Dad. "Drive safe." He grunts his response, and I'm out the door.

At school, the heat has gone out and everyone is wearing their jackets to class. The cold makes it even harder to concentrate, and since Monday classes are always especially soul-sucking, it's a gigantic relief when my afternoon free hour finally rolls around. I often spend the time in the art room, working on my drawings and watching Ms. Twohey, but today I head for the library. I want to go online and see if I can find anything about the incident with Brian's unit.

Half an hour and no luck later, I sign off. My jacket has slipped off the back of my chair and fallen to the floor, and as I reach for it I spot Scarlett sitting at a table across the library. Her jacket is unzipped but she has a scarf wrapped around her neck and enormous mittens on her hands; they look handmade, and I wonder whether her grandma knitted them for her. Even wearing them, she's somehow writing on a piece of notebook paper lying on the table in front of her.

I get up and wander casually across the room, pretending to be searching for a title on the shelves. "Hey, Scarlett," I call softly, pulling a book off the shelf.

She looks up, covering the notebook in front of her with an arm. "Oh … hey," she says. She nods at the book in my hand. "Doing some reading?"

I glance at the title I'm holding. *All About Puberty: What's Going On Down There.* "Well," I say sheepishly, "you can never know too much."

I'm encouraged when she almost cracks a smile. "Writing a letter?" I venture, tossing the book onto a random shelf.

"This is the twenty-first century, dork; nobody writes letters anymore." Scarlett taps her pencil on the paper in front of her but doesn't move her arm. "Just working on some random stuff."

"Oh."

Awkward silence. "Should I bring my stuff over here?" I ask, indicating the vacant chairs at her table.

She shrugs. "Sure."

I ignore the lukewarm response and drop my jacket onto the chair, then go to retrieve my backpack, which I left over by the computers. By the time I get back, Scarlett has returned to her writing and, without conversation, I'm stuck with nothing to do. Reluctantly, I take out my algebra and start halfheartedly doing it. By the time the bell rings at the end of the period, I'm surprised to find I've finished most of the assignment.

"Guess that's it," Scarlett says, closing her notebook.

"Yep," I agree. I assume we'll walk out together, but by the time I finish packing up my books, she's waved and left. *Just another day in Strange Scarlett Land*, I tell myself.

Ten minutes later, I'm settling into a desk in Government class, wondering as usual why I signed up for such a dry subject at the end of the day. As the teacher drones on, I rub my cold hands together to wake up, then slide them into my jacket pockets. In the left one, something pokes my hand, and I pull out a tightly folded square of paper. On it are these words:

Polychrome

The crimson velvet of a lover's rose
The blackness of the sky expecting stars
The silver sheen of tears I've yet to cry
Translucent on their way to heal my scars

The white-gold of a flame about to burn
The grayness of the earth awaiting snow
The blue-green trace of veins beneath my skin
The brilliance of the aching in my soul

The words are beautiful and strange, painful somehow. When the bell rings signaling the end of last period, I refold the paper carefully, and tuck it into my pocket, more curious about Scarlett than ever.

FIFTEEN

....

The way Mom cleans the house in preparation for Brian's return, you'd think she's expecting the President of the United States. From the minute she gets home after work, she's cleaning carpets, hauling boxes of old clothes to the thrift store, and spraying, wiping, or dusting just about everything else. Worse yet, she's recruited me to help; I scoop moldering fall leaves out of the gutters, sweep and power-wash the garage floor despite the cold, and carry endless bags of junk to the curb for the garbage pickup. "Mom, seriously... Brian's not going to care about all this," I tell her, but she just shakes her head at me.

"Dov," she says impatiently, waving me off toward another assignment. "Just do what I ask for once, would you?"

While she starts working on the basement, it suddenly

occurs to Mom that Brian might not even be able to stay in his bedroom down there. "I don't know what I was thinking," she mutters, looking ready to cry. "He probably won't be able to manage these stairs, as banged up as he is. We better put him in your room, at least temporarily," she decides.

"No way," I protest. "I'm not moving all my stuff downstairs."

"Don't be selfish, Dov; it won't be for long. I'm sure that Brian's going to want to get things back to normal every bit as fast as you do."

In the end, we compromise; I agree to sleep in the basement temporarily as long as I can leave Leo's cage in my room upstairs. His appetite seems to be down, and I'm worried about moving him. Still, I make it a point to grumble under my breath as I carry armloads of stuff down the stairs and drop it on Brian's desk, a spot previously reserved for his photographic shrine to Victoria. Mom has moved Victoria's pictures to my room, arranging them carefully on the bedside table. "I'm sure Brian will want to have these where he can see them while he's recuperating," she murmurs.

I almost say that I doubt Brian will spend much time lying in bed, but in the end I keep my opinion to myself. I'm getting back into my invisible mode, in anticipation of my esteemed brother's return.

Brian won't have much need for Victoria's pictures anyway; she's practically moved in with us. If Mom isn't sanitizing the house, she and Victoria are huddled at the kitchen table over cups of Constant Comment, planning the Hallmark Channel special *Brian and Victoria Howard Live Happily Ever After.*

"I hope he's well enough to help me with the wedding planning," Victoria says one day the next week. I'm in the living room, staring at the television and only halfway listening to their voices from the kitchen. "There are so many things we need to decide."

"I'm sure he'll be happy with whatever you want," Mom assures her. "I can't think of a better way to close this terrible chapter in our lives than a beautiful wedding."

Brian asked Victoria to marry him the day before he deployed, giving her a small but sparkling diamond ring he bought with the money he earned working at Scheels Sporting Goods. Victoria has already spoken to Brian's supervisor and reports that Brian can have his job back as soon as he wants it. "He's the best manager Scott's ever had," Victoria tells Mom proudly. "He hasn't been able to find anyone to replace him."

Wow, my brother is irreplaceable. Giant surprise.

"Brian has such an easy way with people," Mom agrees. "He's been that way since he was a toddler. It always puzzled me, because I was such a shy child myself. I guess Dov must take after me ... "

This conversation is becoming entirely too predictable. I slide off the couch so I don't have to hear Victoria say *yes, Dov IS a loser with no social skills,* and head for my room while it's still my room.

From under the mattress, I extract the two folded pieces of paper I hid there, then flop onto my back on the bed and stare at the ceiling, trying to clear my mind. After a minute, I carefully unfold the first one; it's *Polychrome*, the poem I found in my jacket pocket last week. I've unfolded and refolded it so many times the paper has grown thin along the creases. Each time I read the words, they seem to take on a different meaning.

I found the second poem yesterday; when I opened my locker, a folded piece of notepaper was sitting on top of the books, papers, and other detritus that live in the bottom. I knew what it was even before I unfolded it, so I wasn't surprised. It was written in the same neat, even handwriting as *Polychrome*.

I
ache
I
plead
I
scream
I roar
I want
I yearn
I claw the floor
I'm
scared
I'm lost
I've been

Misled
I'm bent
I'm busted
Damaged.
Dead.

It's untitled, but it doesn't need one to communicate the writer's pain. Even the shape the words take on the page makes me picture something sharp and dangerous. Reading it through again, I consider my theory: that it's Scarlett leaving me the poems.

I sigh and lay the poem on my chest. *Scarlett,* I think. The angles of her name in my mind feel as sharp-edged as the words on the paper. Figuring out Scarlett is like putting together a thousand-piece jigsaw puzzle without having any idea of the finished picture. Maybe the poems are Scarlett's way of giving me a picture of what's going on inside of her, even if she can't talk about it.

I've come to realize that Scarlett is determined to hold everyone in Longview at arm's length. Whenever I text her to ask if she wants to hang out, she always has some excuse. At school, she has this weird way of hovering around the fringe of things, being a part of the scenery but always avoiding any chance that the focus might fall on her. I've beckoned her over to our table at lunch and sometimes she joins us, but she sits quietly, nibbling on a piece of fruit and giving one- or two-word responses when anybody tries to include her in the conversation.

"Social phobia" was Miranda's diagnosis when I mentioned it to her, and now she just shrugs and makes it clear that Scarlett is the last person she wants to discuss. Miranda's opinions are as unwavering as the thin black line she draws above her lashes, but I've never known her to be so unwilling to befriend someone. Ali and Koby are neutral toward Scarlett; they can't understand why I go out of my way to try to include someone who so clearly doesn't care to be included.

I'm not even sure myself what it is that's keeping Scarlett on my brain; incredibly, she seems to have taken up at least part of the space previously occupied by Ms. Twohey. Usually, I have no problem with anybody who makes it clear that they want to be left alone. Heck, wanting to be left alone is something I totally get. For some reason, though, thoughts of Scarlett play over and over in my head, like an earworm that has randomly taken up residence in my brain.

I read through *Untitled* once again, then refold it with a sigh. From his vantage point on the dresser, Leo is watching me. "What are we gonna do with you?" I ask him. In the past few days, he's eaten only one cricket, and I'm not even absolutely sure about that. "Help me out here."

But Leo, normally full of sage advice, has little to offer tonight. Instead, as he often does lately, Leo closes his heavy-lidded eyes and drifts off to sleep.

"How about you, guys?" I ask the folks in the Sunny Day Real Estate poster hanging over my bed. The Fisher-Price dad looks like he's about to say something, but the Fisher-Price mom nods toward the burning toaster and he shuts up.

Once again, it seems, I'm on my own.

SIXTEEN

Dad happens to be home again when Brian's doctor calls with an update on his status. From my room, I listen to him run through the list, to Mom, of what he's been told. Brian's concussion has mostly resolved, and his shoulder has been pinned. "He'll have to wear a sling for a while, but that's nothing," Dad says. Brian's ribs are healing on their own, but one of his eyes was badly injured and it's too early to tell the outcome. In the meantime, he'll have to wear an eye patch. I hear Mom give a little *mew* of concern at this piece of news, but something tells me that on Brian, an eye patch and a sling will only make him look cool and pirate-like.

"The doc mentioned that he's suffering from some sort of combat stress," Dad adds.

"Oh dear," Mom murmurs. "I've heard about that."

Dad snorts. "I told him, 'of course he's suffering from combat stress...what he went through would be stressful for anyone.'"

"Yes," Mom agrees. "Of course it would be."

"I told the doc," Dad continues heartily, "that if anybody can man up and put this behind him, it'll be Brian."

Nothing from Mom; even though I can't see her, I can picture the worried crease forming between her eyes again. It was nice not to see that crease for a while.

"Hell," Dad mutters. "Every damned one of us is suffering from combat stress around here, and we weren't even *in* combat."

Things move quickly after that; only a few more days pass until Brian himself calls with the news that he's coming home next Sunday. Mom says his voice is weak, but that he's making sense and sounds good. We all breathe easier, and the mood in the house is the lightest it's been in months.

I also feel better having finished my quarter-term exams. For once, I think I may have done halfway decent on them; I've been putting a little more effort into school lately for reasons I don't really understand. Maybe I feel like I owe somebody something; my brother is coming home alive and there's a chance things might be getting back to normal. I realize that I haven't fully appreciated good old boring "normal" until now.

No one but me has noticed my improved grades; things at home are in full Brian's-coming-home mode and there isn't much attention left over for anything else. Not that I necessarily want my parents' attention focused on me, anyway.

"When my folks get my grades, it's not gonna be good," moans Koby across the lunch table. "Don't be surprised when my dismembered body turns up in the landfill." Koby's parents are notoriously uptight about grades, and Koby seems to do his level best to fail to meet their expectations.

"I *offered* to help you study for that *Red Badge of Courage* exam," Ali reminds him.

"Yeah." Koby nods thoughtfully. "Studying. That would have been good."

"I'll bet you didn't even read the book."

"Sure I did."

Ali looks skeptical. "Really? Give us the Koby *Cliffs Notes*."

Koby clears his throat. "*The Red Badge of Courage*," he begins. "After the long walk through the woods, the Big Bad Wolf jumped out and told Little Red Riding Hood, 'I'm going to take your basket of cherries.' Well, as the title suggests, Red grew a pair and said 'Oh no, Mr. Wolf, don't take my whole basket of cherries!' Then she felt kind of bad for the dude, so she said, 'Here, you can have just one...'"

Ali rolls his eyes. "You don't even know how *that* story goes, moron." There's no need to ask Ali about *his* midterm grades; he probably read *The Red Badge of Courage* while the rest of us were still sounding out *Hop On Pop*.

Miranda is late for lunch, but now she comes hurrying toward the table. "Guess what," she says breathlessly, setting her tray down with a clatter. "My mom was listening to the radio on her way home from the grocery store, and KXLY announced this contest. She called in and she won."

"What's the prize?" I ask curiously.

"That's the thing," Miranda says, smiling. "The prize is ... six tickets to the Poisoned Heart concert."

The table erupts. "*POISONED HEART!*" Ali exclaims over and over, like he isn't sure he's heard right. Poisoned Heart is a sick hardcore band from the Twin Cities and while they're number one on the iTunes download list, they've never played anywhere near Longview before. It's every kid's dream to see them live, at least among my friends.

Miranda tears open a bag of salt-and-vinegar potato chips. "So," she says, "they're playing at the Milford City Coliseum on December 3rd; everyone can go, right?"

"Are you kidding?" Koby demands. "When are we ever going to get another chance to see a band like Poisoned Heart?"

Miranda grins and nods, her mouth full of chips.

"I can drive, if everyone throws in some cheddar for gas," I say. The Gator's a gas hog, but good for road trips when everyone is participating.

"I'll have to let you know," Ali says. His dark eyes dart briefly in my direction; I wonder whether the concert date conflicts with RedWarrior23's honeymoon or something.

"You're coming," Miranda informs him. "No one's missing this."

Ali nods; it appears there's a strong possibility the wedding will be postponed. I hope Moridin is an understanding groom.

"Hey, since you have two extra tickets," I suggest, "how about asking Scarlett if she wants to come along?"

Miranda pokes at her hamburger with a carrot stick. "Boy, you just don't give up on that chick, do you?"

I shrug. "I think she's just…"

"Socially challenged?" Koby suggests.

I frown. "I was going to say, 'going through a lot.' We all know it sucks when people jump to conclusions about you. Seriously, she's cool; you should really give her another chance." I look directly at Miranda. "Ask her to the concert," I challenge. "Do it for me."

Miranda's face flushes. *Don't ask me to do that*, says her expression, but the words that come out of her mouth are, "I'll think about it."

"And count me in," I add. "In fact," I say, throwing my arms around Miranda and pulling her to me in a big side hug, "did I ever tell you that I love you?"

Eventually, even Miranda is laughing. We can't believe it; in a little over a month, we're going to see Poisoned Heart perform live! For the moment, anyway, life is beyond good.

SEVENTEEN

From the moment we see Brian's plane touch down, it's hard to wipe the big cheesy grin of happiness off my face. News of his return somehow got out to the media, so by the time we arrived at Longview Airport, the WDAL news crew was already waiting. I spotted Paul Sturman, local news reporter, admiring his reflection in the airport window; as I watched, he tilted his head and raked his fingers through the front of his hair. All the moms in town think Sturman is Longview's answer to Matt Lauer, and I guess he has a reputation to uphold.

Naturally, Dad came in from the road in order to welcome his favorite son back from war; he barely made it back to town in time to shower, shave, throw on some clean clothes, and drive us to the airport. I overheard Victoria telling Mom that she'd spent all afternoon at the beauty salon, making sure she looked perfect for the first time she sees Brian. I have to admit, she does look great, and she smells like some kind of exotic flower.

Brian's flight's arrival is announced and we all watch anxiously as deplaning passengers come down the stairs and through the gate. For an instant I think about what a fluke it would be if Brian missed his flight, but a moment later it occurs to me how Mom would react if he didn't get off that plane, and I'm glad it won't happen like that.

Among the throng of people exiting the gate area, a soldier in camo-casual makes his way slowly toward us. One arm is hidden inside his jacket, held close to his thin body by a neat, dark sling. A black patch covers one eye, and the other eye looks a little dazed as it scans the crowd.

It's then that I finally know it for sure: my brother is home. Alive. Out of danger. An uneven lump of happiness and relief forms in my throat, and I'm not even embarrassed when I feel tears prickling behind my eyes.

"There he is!" screams Victoria, grabbing my arm. I don't know what it is that makes girls jump up and down when they get excited, but Victoria is definitely a jumper. My arm feels like it's going to be torn off at the shoulder.

On the other side of me, Dad sees Brian too. "There he is, all right," he says to no one in particular, a proud grin stretching across his face. "There's my boy." Mom's already following behind Victoria, who's let go of me and is running toward Brian.

"Here he comes now," Paul Sturman informs the cameraman. "We don't want to miss this … and … we're rolllinggg … "

The camera's big light snaps on just in time to capture the moment when Victoria throws her arms around my brother's neck. Brian is smiling now, but the force of Hurricane Victoria sends him stumbling backwards half a step.

"Oh my God … baby … baby …" Victoria sobs. She doesn't seem to notice that she almost knocked Brian over; she's busy burying her face deep in my brother's neck, "Thank God you're safe!"

Mom stands nearby, her hands clasped together. Tears stream down her face as she waits for her turn to hug her son. When Victoria finally releases him, Brian sees her standing there and opens his arms. Mom moves into them and gives him a long hug. "Brian … oh, Brian," I hear her say. "You can't imagine how we worried."

When it's his turn, Dad salutes him heartily. "Welcome home, soldier," he says, his voice hoarse with emotion. He wipes his eyes quickly, then holds out his hand to pump Brian's. "Good to have you back. Good to have you back," he repeats.

"Glad to be back, sir," Brian nods. He finishes shaking Dad's hand and looks over at me. "What's up, little brother?" He smiles.

"Not much."

"Got a new look, huh?" When Brian deployed nine months ago, my hair was still the color of muddy water, and my wardrobe consisted of saggy jeans and random T-shirts. Apparently no one told him about my reinvention.

"Yeah." I nod, my throat clogging with unexpected

tears. The next thing I know, I'm hugging my brother, gently because of his sling between us.

"Thanks, bro," Brian mutters. "My ribs are still a little sore." Close up, I can see that Brian has tiny scabs all over his face, as if he's been sandblasted.

"Welcome back, Private Howard," Paul Sturman interrupts, pushing a jumbo microphone between us. "We don't want to interrupt your reunion here, but the whole community wants to know how it feels to be back on American soil. Back on your old stomping grounds."

Brian hesitates; he seems overwhelmed by all the commotion. "Well," he says, smiling, "to tell you the truth, it doesn't feel quite real yet, but when it does, it's going to be pretty awesome. Even right now, it would be hard to slap the happy off my face."

Sturman grins. "That's great, just great. Tell us, Brian, what happened over there? How were you injured?"

Brian's eye shifts and he looks uncomfortable. "Well," he says slowly, as if he's remembering, "my unit was out on patrol in Kabul, and we were engaged by insurgents."

"And by 'engaged' you mean attacked," Sturman supplies helpfully.

"Attacked, yeah," Brian agrees. "We were attacked."

"Now, from what I understand, some of the other soldiers in your unit didn't make it back."

"Yessir," Brian says, his voice cracking. "Three brave men and one outstanding woman lost their lives that day."

"Wow," Sturman marvels. "That's extraordinary. We are always so sorry and proud when our brave men and women make the ultimate sacrifice for our country." He pauses for a respectful moment before continuing. "Now, Private Howard, how do you account for your making it through that terrible day alive? When so many other soldiers in your unit were killed?"

My brother's chest lifts as he takes a deep breath; it's a few beats before he exhales. "I don't know," he says faintly. "I guess maybe someone was watching over me?" He breaks eye contact with the reporter and meets mine. "Could I sit down, do you think?" he asks me. "I—I'm feeling kind of shot all of a sudden."

There's a flurry of activity as Brian is ushered to a nearby bank of chairs, Sturman and the cameraman trailing along behind. My brother does look weary as he sinks gratefully onto a chair.

Sensing his subject doesn't have much left to offer, Sturman turns to my parents. "Tell us what you're feeling tonight, Mrs. Howard," he invites.

Mom sighs happily. "Oh, it's so wonderful to finally have him here, home safely. Of course he's got some injuries … he'll need to recover from those … but we're just very grateful to be one of the families fortunate enough to have our soldier come home."

"I imagine you certainly must be," Sturman agrees. The cameraman points to his watch and Sturman turns and looks into the camera. "Here with the very happy family of Longview's own Private Brian Howard," he summarizes, "I'm Paul Sturman for WDAL news."

"And … cut. That's a wrap." The cameraman snaps off

the light. It's a relief to be out of the bright glare, but losing it makes everything feel dull and two-dimensional.

"Thanks so much for letting us intrude on your reunion," Paul Sturman says, handing the microphone to the cameraman without even looking to make sure he's there to receive it. "Didn't mean to interrupt, but it's a great story. Gotta bring the happy news when we can these days."

Dad shakes Sturman's hand again. "I imagine everyone in Longview will be glad to know Brian Howard made it back safely. He was quite an athlete for Longview High, you know."

"Oh, indeed I *do* know," the reporter agrees. "I covered that game against Milford Central. He ran for … "

"For 210 yards," Dad finishes, laughing. "Wasn't that something?"

"It sure was." Sturman looks at Brian, but my brother isn't paying attention. Instead, he's listening to whatever Victoria is whispering into his ear. Distractedly, he shifts position in his chair, then grimaces and reaches his good hand up to touch his ribs.

"Kind of brings it all home to see him come back like this, doesn't it?" the reporter murmurs to Dad, who doesn't reply right away.

"Yes, it does," Dad says finally. "But at least now he'll be able to get on with his life knowing that he did his part. My kid's a real hero in my eyes."

Sturman nods. "He's a hero to us all."

Mom suddenly claps her hands together to get everyone's attention; Brian jumps at the sharp sound, which makes us all laugh.

Mom puts a hand on Brian's shoulder to reassure him. "I'm sorry, sweetheart; I didn't mean to startle you! I was just going to say, 'let's get this show on the road.' Is anyone hungry? I've got a roast in the oven, and sweet potatoes. Apple pie for dessert. All Brian's favorites."

"Wow, Mom," Brian says, "that sounds great. It's been a long time since I've eaten anything that didn't have grit as the main ingredient. I can hardly wait ... in fact, what *are* we waiting for?"

Everyone laughs, including Brian, and begins to make preparations for departure. I trot off and find Brian's duffel bags circling on the baggage carousel, and Mom and Victoria keep Brian company while Dad goes off to pull up the Suburban. Now that we've gotten a look at Brian's condition, Dad wants to give him curbside service.

When I get back with his bags, Mom and Victoria both decide they have to find the restroom before we leave for home. "Keep an eye on my baby," Victoria instructs me, bending down to kiss my brother's clean-shaven cheek. "This is the last time I'm letting him out of my sight."

Brian laughs. "I'm gonna hold you to that," he tells her, hanging onto Victoria's hand until she's out of reach. I can tell how happy he is to see her, and it makes me like Victoria even more.

Mom leans down and kisses a spot just above the place Victoria kissed. "You just rest," she says softly. "We won't be long."

"You'd better not be," Brian agrees. "Now that you've started my stomach growling with all this talk of apple pie."

Mom giggles like a giddy young girl and scurries off after Victoria. I sit down on the chair next to Brian. It's been so long, it feels awkward being alone with him. "So...kinda a lot to take in, huh?" I offer.

"You don't know the half of it, bro...my head is pounding right now. It's kind of like being in some sort of weird dream I had a long time ago."

I nod as if I understand.

Brian sighs. "But really, it's awesome to be back. Nice to take off my boots for the last time."

"Yeah," I chuckle, but I'm thinking about something I saw in his face just before he spoke. Something that suggests that even though Brian feels like he's in a dream, all my brother really wants to do is lie down and fall into a deep and dreamless sleep.

EIGHTEEN

....

On the ride home in the car, it seems like the old Brian is back. With Dad's help, he climbed into the middle seat of the Suburban and slid over next to the window. Victoria, of course, wedged in close beside him, resting her head on his shoulder. With Dad driving and Mom riding shotgun, that leaves me stuck in the third seat with Brian's duffel. All the way home, Mom keeps looking over her shoulder, as if to assure herself that Brian is still there. "Everything's pretty much the same around here," she tells him as we drive past the familiar landmarks of Longview. "Not many changes while you were gone."

"It's not like I've been away for years, Mom," Brian reminds her. He stares out the window as we pass the high school. "Things do look sort of different, though," he comments. "Maybe it's the one-eye thing."

"Or maybe it's you who's changed," Victoria murmurs, smiling up at him.

"Maybe that's it." From behind, I watch as my brother uses his good arm to pull his fiancée close so he can drop a kiss onto her hair.

Main Street is busy for a Sunday night. The sign over the Empire Arts Center advertises the staging of a performance, and on the sidewalk underneath people are milling around before going inside. "Oh look," Mom says. "The Gaither choir is in town."

"What's wrong, babe?" I hear Victoria whisper. I was staring out the window, idly watching the theater crowd as we passed, but now I look at Brian. He's pulled away from Victoria and is glued to the window, staring out into the throng of people as we drive slowly by them, his eyes moving back and forth over the crowd.

"Babe?" Victoria repeats.

"Swing back around," Brian orders, his voice high and tight. "Let's take another run past there."

"What was that, dear?" Mom asks from the front seat. She turns and looks over her shoulder at Brian, a happy, expectant smile on her face.

"Something wrong, Brian?" Dad asks, his eyes on Brian in the rearview mirror.

As we leave the scene behind, Brian follows it with his eyes, then turns back toward the front. "Forget it," he says. "I just, uh, I thought I saw something. I guess there's nothing to worry about here, right?" He sits back against the seat, but the set of his shoulders tells me he hasn't completely relaxed.

Victoria snuggles closer. "You're home now," she soothes. "I'm going to take care of you." I'm glad it's dark so no one can see me roll my eyes.

"Roger that," Brian agrees, smiling. "No worries."

Mom chatters nervously the rest of the way home, doing her best to keep Brian's mind off anything but love, peace, joy, and happiness, and we manage to make the rest of the trip without incident. When Dad pulls into the driveway the car's lights sweep across the front of the house, illuminating the carved Halloween pumpkin waiting on the front steps and the big *WELCOME HOME BRIAN* sign that Mom and Victoria hung across the garage door.

"Now who did that?" Brian asks, sounding pleased.

Victoria plants a kiss on his cheek. "Guess," she prompts.

"Aw, Dov, you made me a sign?" Brian teases. "You're just the *sweetest*!"

"It's the *least* I could do," I agree.

Victoria elbows him. "Ow!" Brian yelps, making Victoria suck in her breath in horror.

"Oh my God, baby, I'm so sorry…"

"Just kidding," Brian laughs. "It's my other side, anyway."

"Jerk!" Victoria socks him, hard. They tussle for a minute, then start kissing.

"Geez," I mutter, already ready for the reunion to be over.

Dad parks and shuts off the engine. "Dov, carry in your brother's duffel," he orders.

"Aye-aye, Sergeant." I pretend not to see the dangerous look my father directs back to me via the rearview mirror.

Mom goes on ahead to check the roast, and the rest of us follow slowly behind her into the house. Brian and Victoria bring up the rear, still clinging to each other.

The minute we get inside the house it becomes clear that something is wrong; the air smells of burnt meat. "Damn, damn, damn ... " Mom can be heard lamenting in the kitchen. A moment later she appears in the doorway of the living room, looking stricken. "Brian," she says, "I was so excited when we left, ... I must have set the oven too high. I'm afraid the roast is ruined."

Dad makes a sound of angry disgust. "Good *God*, Laura," he says. "His first night home ... "

"Hey," Brian interrupts, "that's totally fine, Mom. Please don't worry about it. The truth is, I'm kind of beat anyway. Maybe we could just order pizza or something? I don't think it's going to be too long before I crash out hard."

Mom looks so miserable that I honestly feel sorry for her. "But it's not much of a celebration meal," she protests, sounding defeated.

"You know what?" Brian soothes her the way he always did. "To tell you the truth, Mom, I'm a little relieved. I was thinking that you'd gone to all that trouble and here I was, too shot to even really enjoy it. Maybe we could do the big meal in a few days, once I've had a chance to rest up a little. We can invite Vicki's parents. I promise, we'll celebrate then."

I glance at Victoria, who's looking at my brother like he's hung the moon. Once again I'm reminded of how skilled my brother is at making the people around him happy. In the past I didn't care much, but now I make a mental note to start watching closely; maybe I can learn something.

"That's an awesome idea, babe," Victoria is saying. "I know Mother and Daddy will be thrilled. And you *do* look tired. I'm sure you're exhausted after the trip and all the excitement."

"Oh yes," Mom agrees. "I don't know why we didn't think of that. Mick, why don't you order the pizza? And after that, it's right to bed with you, soldier."

"No mushrooms," I murmur as Dad starts toward the kitchen. Too much like human flesh.

"Don't forget the extra mushrooms," Brian calls, grinning at me.

"Extra mushrooms it is!" Dad agrees without looking back.

I make a face at Brian and show him my middle finger, but I can't keep from grinning back.

"Brian," Mom says, wringing her hands nervously. "I've set you up in Dov's room; I hope that's all right. I just thought it might be tough for you to do the stairs with your ... you know ... injuries."

I look at Mom's anxious face, and in that moment I suddenly understand that it isn't about Brian not being able to walk up and down a few stairs. Really, Mom just wants the son that she's worried, and fretted, and cried countless tears over to be physically close to her—at least until she can believe he's really back home, and safe for good. I imagine she might even get up in the night and walk down the hallway to stand in the doorway of the room, listening in the darkness for the reassuring sound of my brother's breathing.

Whether he's thinking all of this too or just was too tired to object, Brian shrugs. "I guess it's okay with me, as long as Dov doesn't mind."

"No big deal," I assure him. "It will give me a chance to finish reading your diary."

Brian laughs. "Just make sure you skip the sections about Victoria."

"But those are the best parts!"

Grinning, I carry Brian's heavy duffel toward my room; it's killing my shoulder and I'm eager to put it down. I set it on the desk where he can reach it easily, then wander over to say hello to Leo. I've already let him in on the new sleeping arrangements and he's promised to keep an eye on things while Brian is staying in my room.

I was relieved, earlier, to see evidence that the cricket census in the aquarium has decreased a little; I'm hopeful that it means Leo's weird fasting period is coming to an end. He even looks a little better, I think; his coloring seems brighter, and he seems to have more energy.

"Like we discussed earlier, Brian's going to be bunking with you temporarily," I tell him. "That's no excuse to go on another starvation diet. Other than that minor detail, everything else is going to remain normal around here."

What's your definition of "normal," Grasshopper? Leo asks dryly.

I look at my brother's greenish-gray duffel, the words *Pvt. B.Howard* stamped officially on the side with military precision. On the wall behind the duffel hangs my *Folie à Deux* poster—a picture of a bear piggybacking on a person wearing a bear suit.

I glance back at Leo, who's waiting patiently for my reply. "Point taken," I sigh.

NINETEEN

(The Intelligencer)—An upper-level US official in Afghanistan has resigned to protest a war he says cannot be won. Meanwhile, six more US troops died yesterday, making this the second deadliest month in the multi-year conflict.

....

When I wake up the next morning, it takes me a few minutes to realize where I am. I peer blearily around the dim room before I realize I'm in Brian's bedroom. My brother is home, and he's sleeping upstairs in mine.

It's chilly in the dank basement, and I snuggle further down under the blankets while I finish waking up. The sounds down here are different ones than I'm used to: the tick of the old furnace, the creaking of the foundation, the muffled voices from overhead. It's Monday, but with the news of Brian's homecoming I've been given permission to go to school late. It's great to imagine everyone else sitting in class while I'm still lying in bed. I savor it for a few more minutes, before the rumbling of my stomach and the deep sound of my father's voice prompt me to trudge reluctantly up the stairs.

"Well, would you look what crawled up from the cellar this fine Halloween morning?" Dad says. "One of the zombies from *Night of the Living Dead.*"

"Mick," Mom tsks disapprovingly. "Would you like some breakfast, Dov? I saved you some bacon."

"Sure."

"Morning," Brian says. He's sitting at the kitchen table in the same old chair where he always sat.

I drop into mine, stifling a yawn. A few minutes later, Mom puts a plate of eggs and bacon in front of me; it smells fantastic and I waste no time digging in.

Brian's reading the paper. "Suicide bombing in Pakistan," he informs me, refolding the paper. "Fucking jihadists."

"Brian!" Mom exclaims, shocked, for once, by the Golden Boy.

"Oh, relax, Laura," Dad says, stubbing out his cigarette. "He's a grown man."

My mouth is full of food, which makes it easy to stay out of the conversation.

"How'd you sleep downstairs, Dov?" Mom asks from the sink where she's drying breakfast dishes. She seems unusually concerned about me this morning.

"Great," I tell her. Despite the excitement of Brian's homecoming, the heavy darkness of the basement made it easy to fall asleep.

"Brian says he didn't sleep very well in your room," she comments. "I wonder if you need a new bed."

New bed or not, I figure this means that I'll be back in my old digs before too long.

"I told you, Mom, it had nothing to do with the bed," Brian says. "My sleep has sucked lately. From what I hear, lots of guys have problems sleeping when they get off deployment. Quit worrying; it's such a little thing."

Mom turns and swats at Brian with the damp dishtowel. "Listen here, mister," she says, smiling. "You just let your old mother worry about *little things* right now. I'm kind of enjoying it."

Brian raises his hands in mock surrender. "All right," he agrees. "Worry away."

"Thank you." Mom swats him once more with the towel for good measure.

"So," Brian says to me, "you ditching school today?"

"Just taking my time getting there."

"Sweet."

"What about you, Brian?" Mom asks. "Is there anything you want to do today?"

"Victoria's coming by to pick me up around noon; she wants me to come by and say hello to her family. I might swing by Scheels and let them know I made it back okay."

I finish my breakfast while the three of them make small talk, then head into my room to find some clothes. Sheba is there, lying in a patch of fall sunlight on my neatly made bed. Up until Mom changed the sheets for Brian, my bed hadn't been made in weeks; I'm sure Sheba mistakenly thought she was in a different room.

"Out," I tell her, and make a quick, threatening move that sends her lunging for the hallway.

When I'm dressed, I stop by the aquarium to say good morning to Leo. He's partially submerged in his pool, asleep with his chin resting on the edge of one side while his tail drapes across the other. This is odd; Leo sometimes takes a quick dip, but I've never seen him actually *lying* in the pool before. He looks ... dead.

"Hey," I say, my heart starting to beat faster. "Buddy." Quickly, I lift the cover and reach in to give Leo a nervous poke with my finger. To my relief, he comes to life, scrambling out of the water and over to his warming rock. "Don't scare me like that," I scold.

Don't scare ME like that, he retorts.

On the way to school, I hear the DJ on XL-93 announcing the Poisoned Heart concert. "Tickets are going fast," he warns. "Get 'em while they're hot!"

"Already got ours," I reply.

Second period has just ended, so the halls are full. I'm getting my books out of my locker when Scarlett shows up. "Hey," she says. "I didn't think you were here today. Thought maybe you'd started your trick-or-treating early."

I'm surprised she noticed. "Naw, just came in late," I tell her, shutting my locker door.

"So, your brother made it home finally? I saw it on the news last night."

"Yup." We start down the hall, Scarlett walking alongside me. No more poems have found their way into my backpack, pockets, or any other unexpected places lately.

"What's up with you?" I ask her.

"Not much. My dad's doing a little better. At least that's what my mom says."

"Maybe you'll be able to go home by Thanksgiving." I don't want her to miss the concert, but I know that being back with her family is what Scarlett wants.

She shrugs. "Mom says he's not ready to see me yet. Who knows how long it'll be?"

"That sucks."

"No kidding."

"Hey, people." Koby throws his arms around our shoulders from behind. "Whassup?"

"Not much," I tell him, sort of relieved that it's true. "My brother's home."

"Yeah, I saw it on the news last night. Looks like his arm got kinda jacked up?"

"Not too bad. He'll be okay."

Koby turns to Scarlett. "Miranda told you about the concert?"

She nods. "I'll have to ask my mom if it's okay, but I think it will be. She wants me to get to know people here…make friends, you know."

I'm pleased to hear that Miranda decided to invite Scarlett to the concert after all. It'll be a good opportunity for everyone to get to know Scarlett better.

"Awesome," Koby says. "Poisoned Heart…man. Whoever would have thought we'd get to see them play live?"

Scarlett stops walking; we've reached her third period class. "This is me," she tells us.

"See you at lunch?"

Scarlett shakes her head. "I have a doctor's appointment at eleven. I probably won't be back in time. But listen—how about if I give you a call tonight?"

"Sure…" I ignore Koby, who's grinning at me like a monkey. "That'll work."

Scarlett's perfect lips curve up in a smile. "All right," she says. She holds up her cell phone. "I've got your number."

"Yeah." I have to admit it… maybe she does.

TWENTY

·····································

When I get home from school, Brian is sitting on the sofa waiting for me. "Finally," he says in a low voice, grabbing his jacket. "Let's get the hell out of here for a while."

"Huh?" I was planning on taking a nap, but now I drop my backpack on the floor next to the front door.

"I'm going out, Ma!" Brian calls, already heading out the door.

Mom's voice calls back from somewhere in the house. She sounds worried. "What? But where are you going? I've got…"

Brian shuts the door behind us, cutting her off.

"I thought you said Victoria was picking you up?"

"I must have gotten it wrong. Turns out she has class today."

I keep forgetting that Victoria is a freshman at the university. "Uh, sure," I say. "Whatever."

As we approach the car, Brian exhales a deep sigh of relief. "Mom is driving me nuts, man. She's been following me around all day, trying to get me to eat and talking to me in her 'sweet' voice." Mom's sweet voice is the voice she uses when either one of us is sick. Since she's taking the week off work to take care of Brian, I imagine he'll be hearing a lot of it.

"Couldn't Victoria skip class?" I ask. I'm surprised she didn't insist on it.

"She says she's already missed a lot getting ready for me to come home, and she can't afford to skip any more."

"You want to drive?" I offer, holding up the keys.

"Naw." Brian waves them away. "I'd better ride shotgun. Between my arm and this gimpy eye, I don't trust myself yet."

Carefully, he opens the passenger door with his left hand and slides awkwardly inside, trying not to use his rib muscles. Once in, he can't shut the door, and I have to run around and do it for him. "Goddamn," he says when I get behind the wheel. "Everything seems so much harder now."

I don't really know what to say, so I put the key in the ignition, start the engine, and back the Gator down the driveway. As I do, I catch a glimpse of Mom watching from behind the curtains and give her a wave. *Drive carefully*, she warns me telepathically. *We don't want anything to happen to your brother. Oh ... or you either, Dov.*

"Where to?" I ask Brian.

"Just drive. It's nice not to have anyone hovering over me for a little while."

"Dad too?"

Brian nods. "If I have to hear him call me 'soldier' one more time…"

I laugh. "They're just so glad you're back. Seriously, dude, you have no idea what a wreck Mom's been since you left. Then, when we *did* hear…"

"Yeah. I know."

"I mean, geez, Brian…of course everyone was worried that maybe you weren't going to come back at all."

Brian nods, silent. I drive carefully; even though it's not yet five, the smallest trick-or-treaters are already starting to come out.

"You know," he says finally, "I never realized it before I left, but dying isn't necessarily the worst thing that can happen to a person. Sometimes living can be worse."

I *don't* know, actually, and I turn his words over in my head as I slow the Gator to approach an intersection where a tiny princess, a ladybug, and a growth-stunted Spider-Man are crossing.

"You know what I could go for?" Brian says suddenly, interrupting what I'm about to say. He looks over at me. "A taco grinder."

"I could eat," I agree.

Fifteen minutes later we're at the Pepper and I'm balancing two paper plates full of food as we leave the counter. "Follow me," Brian says, gesturing toward the back. He slides into one side of the booths and sits sideways, his back against the wall. He scans the place with his eyes once, then a second time.

I set his food down in front of him, then go back for our drinks. "Thanks, bro," he says when I slide into the other side of the booth. "You don't know how many times I craved the food from this place while I was over there."

I watch as he tries to attack his food, only to discover that handling a full-sized grinder one-handed ... left-handed to boot ... is more challenging than either of us anticipated.

"Here," I say finally. "Let me cut it up or something."

"Thanks," Brian says gratefully after I manage to cut his sandwich into rough but manageable hunks using a plastic knife. He takes his first bite. "Holy crap," he mutters, chewing. "*So* good."

"Can't beat the Pepper."

"Nope."

We inhale our food, not talking, then both sit back to digest. Brian lets out a mighty belch, and I answer it with one of my own.

"So, Bri," I say, "were you ever like ... you know, *scared* over there?"

Brian reaches for his soda and takes a sip. "Was I ever scared?" He considers. "A better question would probably be whether I ever *wasn't* scared. It's a whole different world over there, Dov. Not just the mountains, or the people, their whole culture, but ... I mean ... being out on patrol and getting *shot* at, not knowing whether your unit is going to drive over an IED. You seriously don't know whether you'll even make it through the day."

"Whoa."

Brian nods. "You live every moment knowing there's a chance you might die. It does something to you. How could it not?"

I nod and reach for my soda; listening to Brian, my mouth is suddenly dry.

"When you see guys you live with day in and day out ... when you see them *die*, it really messes you up, you know? Like, you start to wonder whether God even exists."

"Damn."

Brian inhales deeply, like he's found himself suddenly short on air. "Yeah. Exactly."

He pokes at the few bits of shredded lettuce left on his plate. "Heck," he says. "We lost our first CO, Sergeant Wilkie, two weeks after I got there."

"Lost him? Killed, you mean?"

Brian nods. "This young kid had been hanging around our unit for a few weeks; his name was Rahim, and he was probably around ten or eleven. He seemed like a cool kid; heck, we'd hook him up with Cokes and candy bars and let him listen to our music ... for some reason, that kid loved Eminem. The only English he knew was stuff like 'P. Diddy' and 'bling, bling' and 'yo momma'; shit like that. It was pretty hilarious." Brian laughs bitterly. "We kinda got used to having him around, you know?"

I nod.

Brian takes another deep breath. "So things started to kind of heat up in the area and one day my unit heads out on patrol. We make it to town and decide to leave the Bradley and do a foot patrol. We're all moving along, checking to see what's up, and all of the sudden, Rahim shows up. He's got this donkey with him, just a ratty, skinny old donkey with a pack on its back; kind of a riot, you know? So the bunch of us are laughing, and Rahim's trying to bring his donkey over to us, but the damn thing is acting all funny and digs in its heels, like it's spooked or something.

"Once the donkey makes it clear that it's not going anywhere, Rahim starts calling for us to come over and check out his donkey where it's standing, but radio transmissions are coming in and so we have to try to listen to them because we're working, right? The transmission is about some kind of activity up ahead and we really need to get moving over there, but Rahim's having a hissy fit because we won't come see his donkey, so finally Sergeant Wilkie motions us to go on. He heads on over to deal with Rahim himself, to make him understand that it wasn't a convenient time for us to admire his donkey and what not. And wouldn't you know it, the rest of us aren't thirty yards away when suddenly there's this enormous blast and all hell breaks loose."

"W-what happened?" I ask, confused. "Someone shot Wilkie?"

Brian shakes his head. "No, Dov, it was the fricking *donkey*," he says. "The donkey blew up."

"What?!"

"The damn thing was loaded with explosives, and someone had made Rahim lure Sergeant Wilkie over there and blew all three of 'em up. He was trying to get the rest of us over there too, but Wilkie was the only one who took the hit."

"Holy crap. Why would he do that?"

Brian shakes his head. "I don't know what they must have done to the poor kid to convince him to do that. He loved us, you know what I mean? I'm a pretty good judge of character, and I just ... man ... " Brian swallows. "He was just a little kid."

"Yeah."

"And the worst part of it was that once the dust settled, we had to carry the body of our CO ... the *pieces* of his body ... to where we'd left the Bradley, and ride with it all the way back to camp. I'll never forget that, bro; he was just like ... like a pulp. And the smell; the smell of blood and his burned ... I couldn't get that smell out of my head for days."

Brian pushes the plate with the rest of his grinder away; my own stomach is clenched too.

"Damn, Brian," I manage finally, shaking my head. There are so many horrifying things about Brian's story that I can't find the words to speak. "That just ... "

"Sucks," my brother supplies. "We actually have a saying over there that pretty much captures it: *Embrace the suck.*"

"Embrace the suck," I echo.

Brian nods. "It means that when bad shit like that happens, shit that sucks *so* bad you don't even know how to react to it ... well, all you can really do is just kind of take it in, deal with it, and move on."

I guess that's one way people handle stuff they can't quite wrap their minds around.

It's a lot to ponder as we head out to the car. I realize as we walk toward the Gator that even though he doesn't say anything, Brian's eyes are scanning the parking lot as if he expects to see a suspicious vehicle coming over the rise at any moment. I open the car door for him and watch him get inside … my brother who has felt the dark, coppery tentacles of death winding their way up through his nostrils to sear their impression forever into his brain.

On the drive home, Brian is quiet. Daylight has faded to almost nothing, and the trick-or-treaters are out in droves now. We pass the football field. "Hey, look—you had some great runs on that field," I remind him. I'm hoping to take his mind off of everything he's just told me.

Brian stares out the window. "That all seems like it happened a million years ago. Another lifetime in an alternative universe."

"Playing the role of Master of the Universe," I jokingly intone in a movie announcer voice, "Brian Howard!"

Brian chuckles without humor. And now," he says faintly, "I've been cast as Rip Van Winkle. Hey, where am I and what happened to real life?"

Neither one of us says anything more the rest of the way home.

MISSING!

Brian Howard (aka Rip) Last seen wandering outside of his village 20+ years ago. Age progression analysis suggests he might now have a long white beard and a confused, sleepy expression. Reward offered! If found, please contact his concerned brother Dov (aka Not Even a Close Second) Howard.

TWENTY-ONE

....

Mom's agitated when Brian doesn't have much appetite for her Halloween dinner, but we both know better than to mention our after-school meal at the Pepper. After we finish eating (interrupted frequently by the doorbell), I hang out with Leo for a while, straightening up his enclosure. To my surprise, when I lift his cave, I discover the husklike corpses of two crickets. But Leo hadn't eaten them like I'd hoped; instead, they probably starved to death themselves. With a sigh, I remove the crispy, weightless things and reposition the cave, then drop a couple fresh crickets into the enclosure. It looks like things aren't going to work out quite so simply after all.

Just as I'm replacing the cover on Leo's aquarium, my cell phone rings. "Hello?" I answer distractedly.

"Hi, Dov." Scarlett's voice is in my ear.

Despite being worried about Leo, the sound of her voice lifts my spirits. I forgot she said she might call. "Hey. What's up?" I ask.

"Not much. Anything going on with you?"

"Naw. I'm just trying to figure out what to do about my gecko. He's developed some kind of eating disorder." I glance over at Leo, who's lying listlessly in front of the opening to his cave. It's scary how exposed and vulnerable he suddenly looks there.

"Well," Scarlett jokes, "I know a little about eating disorders, but nothing about lizards."

"Thanks anyway," I agree miserably.

"Did you look on the Internet?" Scarlett asks. "There must be some kind of lizard site where you can find out what's wrong."

"Not yet," I admit. "Up until now, I wasn't sure there was really a problem."

Talking about Leo only makes me more worried. I decide it's time to change the subject. "So, you talk to your mom about the concert yet?"

"Not yet. I usually call her before I go to bed, so I'll mention it to her tonight."

"It's gonna be so sweet. I never thought I'd get to see them live."

"Yeah," Scarlett agrees. "I hope I can go. My family is just kind of, you know, overprotective. Especially right now. But I'll ask."

"Okay."

I decide to go out on a limb. "So, I thought a lot about

all that stuff you told me. You know … when we were at the Pepper. Pretty intense."

On the other end of the line, I hear Scarlett sigh. "Yeah," she says, "It's complicated."

"Look," I tell her, "I'm not trying to be nosy, but maybe if you let other people know about what's going on, too, it might help. Miranda, for instance. I mean, she's a girl. She'll get it. Sometimes talking about this stuff can be a good thing."

"Apparently that's why I have to meet with Kerr every other minute."

"I suppose."

"I mean, he's not a jerk or anything, but if I just don't want to talk about it, why can't that be okay?"

I'm silent. I don't know, really, why it all feels so important. I just really like Scarlett, and I want my friends to know her like I do. She's created a barrier, but I'm anxious to help everyone move past it.

"Look," I say. "You don't have to tell people anything you don't want to, obviously. It's just that sometimes, talking about things *does* help a person feel less … alone."

"Why do you think I'm talking to you?"

"Oh … yeah."

"Is that what you do, Dov?" Scarlett ask. "Talk to your friends about, you know, your brother, and your parents, and all the crap in your life?"

She has me there. "Not really," I admit. "Or at least not all of it. But maybe that's part of why I hang around with Ali and Koby and Miranda. Because even if we don't talk about everything wrong with our lives, at least we know that we're with other people who are dealing with some of the same sort of crap. And if we're not alone, it's easier to … embrace the suck."

"Embrace the suck?" she echoes.

"It's, uh, something my brother says." Come to think of it, the phrase does kind of capture the common link between me and my friends. Together, we *embrace the suck* … take what life has dished out to us, deal with it, and move forward in spite of it all.

"I have to admit, I kind of dig it," Scarlett says. She's quiet for a minute. "Look, Dov, I'll make sure I can go to the concert. And I promise I'll try harder with your friends. Okay?"

I can't ask for more. "Yeah," I tell her. "Okay."

After we hang up, I'm lying on the floor of my room paging through my history book and actually reading a few of the words when Dad appears in the doorway of my room. He told Mom he was going to try and spend more time at home, but having him around more is hard to get used to. "Hey," I say, caught off guard.

Dad nods. "I was just talking to your brother about heading up north to do some hunting the weekend after next," he says. "Season opens next weekend, you know."

I nod, although the opening of hunting season isn't exactly something I've marked on my calendar. In fact, I wonder what *any* of this has to do with me.

"I figure by then he'll be fit enough to go and it'll be

good to get him out," he continues. "Remind him that shooting can be for fun, too."

"Sure." If you ask me, it's unlikely that Brian will be able to do a lot of hunting, banged up like he is. Hunters are like mail carriers, though; nothing stops them.

"Your brother suggested we invite you this year," Dad says. "You can help carry Brian's gear."

Thanks a lot, Brian. "Hunting's really not my kind of thing, Dad," I say slowly. "Maybe one of Brian's buddies should go instead. Don't some of them hunt?"

"Your brother wants *you* to come," Dad tells me, making it clear that it wasn't his idea. "I think you can do that for him. You need to man up on this one. God knows Brian's done enough for you."

I try again. "Are you sure he should even *go* this year?" I ask. "I mean, he just barely got back."

"Are you kidding me? The kid can hardly wait. And who knows?" Dad says. "Maybe you'll enjoy yourself." He hoists an invisible rifle to his shoulder and points it straight at me. "PKCHEW!" he says, pulling the trigger.

I picture myself tramping through stubble fields in the predawn cold, my nose running like a faucet as the icy wind burns my face and my entire body slowly morphs into a Dov-shaped icicle.

"Sure," I agree faintly. "Maybe I'll enjoy myself. You never know."

Dad heads off, leaving me to mutter to myself in frustration. At least the big hunting trip doesn't conflict with the weekend of the Poisoned Heart concert. I doubt Dad would think the concert is important enough to get me out of playing gun-mule.

"Well, you know what they say," I mutter to no one in particular as I slam the cover of my history book and toss it across the floor. *Embrace the suck.*

TWENTY-TWO

*(CNN)—The U.S. military suffered another
day of heavy losses in Afghanistan on Friday as
roadside bombs killed four soldiers. An Afghan
civilian working as an interpreter with NATO
troops also was reportedly killed in the attacks.
According to initial reports, both blasts
took place just outside Kandahar...*

....

I'm still fuming about the hunting trip when I get home
from school on Friday and find Brian sitting in front of
the television, trolling through channels in case there's any
coverage on Afghanistan. This has become a routine for
him lately; it reminds me of the days when Mom used to
do the same thing, her nose two inches from the screen in
hopes of catching a glimpse of Brian.

When he sees I've arrived, Brian reaches for his jacket,
which is lying on the couch. "I've been waiting for you,"
he says. "I need you to take me somewhere."

"Just let me get something to eat," I tell him, heading toward the kitchen.

"We'll grab something on the way." Brian is already on his feet, gesturing toward the door.

I'm surprised Brian isn't spending more time with Victoria, having her take him wherever he needs to go. Instead, he seems to prefer to rely on me. Every time I feel annoyed at having to drive Brian somewhere, my dad's words pop into my brain: *Man up...your brother's certainly done enough for you.*

Outside, Brian's already climbed into the passenger seat and is trying to reach across with his good arm to slam the door. "What's the rush?" I ask, closing it for him.

Through the window, I see Brian let out a holler. "AAAAAAAHHHH!" he bellows at the top of his lungs.

I pull the door back open. "What the *hell*, dude?" I demand.

Brian shakes himself. "You have no idea how jumpy I feel today, bro. All day long, it's been like I could crawl out of my skin, for real."

"Well, chill a little," I tell him. "You're freaking me out."

Brian holds up his hands. "Let's go, bro! Let's go, bro!" He repeats it like a mantra until I slam the door again and stomp around to the driver's side, shaking my head.

Once we're out of the driveway Brian focuses on giving me directions. "Turn here," he says, pointing. "Take a right at the next corner."

I don't argue. We cruise toward downtown, where he

gestures for me to pull into the parking lot of Hval's Liquor Store.

"Are you serious, Brian?" I ask when I realize where we are.

"Sure. Why not?"

I gesture toward the sign on the glass door of the liquor store. "Uh, because I'm a *minor*, douchebag. And in case you've forgotten, so are you. They're not going to sell us anything."

Brian makes a face. "You're half right, little brother," he tells me. "We're both minors. But there's one important difference between you and me."

"Oh, I can think of more than one," I mutter.

"I may be a minor," he continues, "but I'm a minor who's also *a veteran*."

"You think that's going to change the birth date on your driver's license?" I ask him. "It's against the law for them to sell to you. Plus, since when do you buy booze, anyway?" I know that before he left for Afghanistan, Brian drank a beer or two with his friends on occasion, but it wasn't something he did regularly. And I've never known him to try and walk into a liquor store and buy.

"Bro," Brian tells me, "some days … like *today*… I just need something to take the edge off. If you were in my shoes … if you *knew* the things that go through my head all day … you'd totally get it. I promise."

"What do you mean, 'the things that go through your head all day'?"

Brian opens his mouth to answer, then shrugs. "You

know what, buddy?" He reaches up to run a hand over his freshly buzzed crew-cut. "Some things are just better not said out loud."

Something in those words sends a chill down my spine, but Brian doesn't give me any time to think about it.

"Come on," he says, pulling the door handle. "I won't be able to carry it myself."

I trail him uneasily into Hval's, anticipating the humiliation of being asked to leave at any moment. Longview is a conservative town, and businesses are regularly fined for selling alcohol or cigarettes to minors. There's virtually no chance this little field trip will end well.

I've never actually been inside a liquor store before, and despite my discomfort, it's impressive to see the shelves of glossy bottles, row after row of colorful labels.

"Hey," Brian says to the guy behind the front counter. The man's eyes travel over Brian and his military haircut, then move on to me, evaluating. Whatever the guy thinks of Brian, I know it's pretty obvious that I'm not twenty-one, and according to the door, my very presence on the premises can cost the establishment two hundred and fifty big ones.

I expect Brian to head toward the back of the store, where cases of beer are stacked waist-high, but he takes a detour down an aisle to the right. Once he finds what he's looking for, he points, gesturing for me to lift down a large, economy-sized bottle of clear liquid from the shelf just below the top. "Vodka?" I demand under my breath. "You're nuts."

"You're right," he agrees, pointing to a second bottle.

"I'd rather have Jack Daniels, but the 'rents would be able to smell that."

I don't know what to say, just pull down the second bottle and follow him to the counter.

The clerk straightens, looking as if he's sizing us up for the confrontation to come. "You fellows find what you need?" he asks me as I set the bottles on the counter.

Wordlessly, I back away. This is Brian's deal, not mine.

"Yep," my brother says, reaching for his wallet. "That oughtta do it."

"Got identification?"

And here we go, I think. I picture our parents being called, who will of course blame me. *Why would you take your brother to a liquor store?* Mom will ask accusingly. *I don't care if he asked you to. You should know he's in a fragile state. He needs your support Dov; I would expect you to have a little more sense, but maybe that's too much to ask...*

One-handed, Brian pulls out his wallet and lays it on the counter so he can shuffle through it. Instead of pulling out his driver's license, he produces his military ID and drops it in front of the clerk.

The man picks it up and studies it, then glances back at Brian. "Vet?" he asks.

"Yessir," Brian replies sharply. "Just got back from the Afghanistan, in fact."

"Army?"

Brian nods. "National Guard."

"Some folks call you guys 'weekend warriors.' Doesn't

exactly strike me as fair. Once you get over there, you're dodging the same artillery as the rest."

I see Brian's face grow hard, but he keeps silent.

"Hey," the man says, realizing. "Weren't you the kid on the news the other night?" Something in his gruff voice grows softer. "Sounds like you were involved in some serious shit."

Brian swallows. "Yessir," he agrees. "Some serious shit."

The clerk's eyes fall on me. "Who's this character, your bodyguard?"

"My brother, sir."

The clerk hands Brian's military ID back to him. Glancing at the door, he pulls out a brown paper bag and put the bottles into them. "Tell ya what," he says, holding the bag toward me. "This one's on me."

My mouth falls open. Wordlessly, I accept the paper bag with the clinking bottles inside.

"That's not necessary," Brian tells him sincerely. "I have money right here … "

The man waves us away. "Nope," he says. He lifts his shirt sleeve and shows us an eagle insignia tattooed on his shoulder. "Vietnam. Two tours. Had to lean on the bottle a little myself after I got back. The least I can do is buy another soldier a drink." He holds out his hand and Brian shakes it, staring wordlessly into the man's face as something significant travels through the air between them.

"Now get your kid brother out of here before the cops stop by," the man says gruffly. "I could lose my license."

When we get out to the car, I let out the breath I've

been holding. "I can't believe it," I say, "Not only did he sell to us, we got it for free!"

Brian pulls one of the bottles from the bag I put on his lap and hands it to me so I can unscrew the cap. "Just so you know, you're not drinking any of it," he informs me. "You're too young." I hand it back and watch as my brother takes a long swallow, then a second. The sweet, sharp aroma of alcohol reaches my nose, and I wonder if Brian really thinks Mom won't be able to smell it.

"Drive," my brother orders, leaning back against his seat with the vodka bottle resting against his chest.

So I do.

TWENTY-THREE

*(AP)—An Army sergeant who arrived home recently
was shot and killed after opening fire on police
officers in Detroit Monday evening. The victim's wife
told authorities that the man had been depressed and
suffering symptoms of post-traumatic stress disorder
since returning from a one-year deployment,
and that earlier in the day he had sent her a
text message reading "I want to die..."*

....

As the weekend of the hunting trip approaches, my dread
and indignation at the whole idea grows stronger. It's only
one item on a long list of sacrifices I've made since Brian
came home. Other items include giving up my bedroom
temporarily, sitting through a soul-sucking dinner with Victoria and her parents, and driving Brian wherever he needs
to go. I've more than done my part, as far as I'm concerned.

It makes no sense that Brian wants me to go hunting
with him and Dad. Mr. Popularity has a thousand friends,
doesn't he? Why can't one of them go instead of me? Then

I realize: aside from a couple "welcome home" get-togeth-ers, Brian hasn't spent much time with his friends since he's been back. True, quite a few of his high school buddies left town after graduation, but some of them are still around. I wonder whether, like me, they're wondering why Brian never calls them or wants to get together. He seems content to spend his time hanging around the house, sleeping, following U.S. troops coverage online, or holing up in the basement to watch slasher flicks with Victoria.

"Baaaaabe ... why can't we rent something I want to see for a change? Does it always have to be those terrible movies?" I heard her asking Brian one day when they were heading off to Blockbuster for another supply. "It doesn't have to be a chick flick ... how about a comedy? You always used to like those."

"Sure." Brian shrugged. "I guess." But when they came back, they'd rented *Saw III* and *American Psycho*. "Brian said everything else looked boring," Victoria explained, rolling her eyes at me.

At school, at least, things have improved. Scarlett has finally relented and started eating lunch with us at the desig-nated emo table. "How many emo kids does it take to change a light bulb?" Ray Sellers calls from two tables over. "Three— one to change the light bulb and two to write a poem about how much they miss the old one!" Ray and his friends crack up, and I see a few kids at other tables laughing too.

"What's his name?" Scarlett asks Koby.

"Ray," he tells her. "Ray Sellers."

Scarlett turns in her chair. "Hey, kid," she calls.

Ray looks over. "Yeah? What do you want?"

"Why don't you shut up and give that hole in your face a chance to heal?" Scarlett yells.

Ooooh ... the sound sweeps across the lunchroom, accompanied by a few snickers. Even Miranda looks impressed.

Ray grins, but his face grows red. "You're pretty hot for an emo kid," he says. "Meet me after school and I'll show you *my* razorblade."

Scarlett considers. "Thanks," she says, "but I don't hang out with people whose parents are cousins."

Oooh, it comes again.

"Burn, sizzle, fry," Miranda murmurs, a small smile of admiration on her face.

Scarlett and Ray stare each other down until Ray can't take it anymore. "Freaky emo bitch," he mutters to his friends, all of whom have suddenly become extremely interested in their lunches.

Scarlett shrugs and turns back to the table. "What a waste of skin." She picks up a carrot stick and begins to chew on it.

"Gotta admit," Koby tells her, offering Scarlett a high five, "you're pretty much my hero right now."

Scarlett hesitates, then brings her palm to his. "Anytime." She smiles.

"So anyway," Miranda says. "Poisoned Heart. Less than a month away."

"It's going to be awesome," Ali agrees. Even he's excited about the concert, and it's hard to get Ali excited about anything that happens in the real world. For better or for worse, things fizzled between RedWarrior23 and Moridin once Ali decided to break the news that he was really a guy from Longview. "I had to come clean," Ali explained to me. "Who wants a marriage that's based on a lie?" Whether it makes sense or not, Ali is now free, and able to come to the concert with the rest of us.

Scarlett's mom has decided she can come along as well. "Hearing that I have some friends probably makes her feel less guilty," Scarlett said, and it was hard not to notice the bitterness in her voice.

Scarlett and I are talking a lot lately; most nights, I fall asleep with the phone under my pillow having just hung up from one of our marathon conversations. She's less enthused about getting together in person; her grandparents like her around in the evenings, she says, and even when I point out to her that they go to bed at eight thirty, she says she doesn't feel right leaving them. I'm starting to suspect she might have a boyfriend back where she comes from.

I told Koby that Scarlett and I are talking a lot. "Does Miranda know?" was his first question, which I thought was strange. The truth is, I haven't mentioned it to Miranda, although I'm not sure why. She's become friendlier toward Scarlett, but I wouldn't say the two of them are friends. Girls are complicated, I've realized.

And to make things even more confusing, I found another poem on Monday, stuffed into the front pocket of my backpack.

An infant, filled with trust
My world the view from your shoulder
Warm milk, soft blankets
Nights spent cradled in loving arms

A tiny child, feeling safe
My world the grass tickling my bare feet
Melting popsicles on wooden sticks,
Dreamless nights in my innocent bed

A young teen, safe no more
World turned on end
Paper shelter, fragile, useless
Falling asleep with tears on my cheeks

Now the future, weary, damaged
The world a cold and foreign place
Eyes wide open, skeleton soul
I lie awake with my ruined heart

Thinking about the words, I sigh. My nightly conversations with Scarlett are nice, but something stops me short of asking her about the poems. They're like a one-sided conversation going on underneath all the other ones we're having.

"I think Miranda wants to be more than friends with you," Scarlett says one night. "I can tell by the way she looks at you."

"Naw," I respond immediately. "I don't think so."

"Who does she like, then?"

I consider, ruling out Koby and Ali almost immediately. She never talks about anyone else, not that I'm the person Miranda would confide in about her love life.

"No one, I guess."

"Uh-huh," Scarlett says knowingly.

"How about you?" I venture. "Anyone back home?"

Scarlett sighs. "No, no one. It's the last thing I'm looking for, believe me. Life is too complicated as it is right now. In case you haven't noticed, I'm barely able to handle friendships."

Ordinarily, I might be disappointed to have been put in the friend zone by Scarlett, but the truth is that my own life seems to be filling up with complications too.

As if the looming hunting trip, Leo's lack of appetite, and the random poetry bombs aren't enough, I have something new to think about: Last night, I woke up with a sudden craving for a bowl of cereal. I headed out to the kitchen and was pouring milk into the bowl when I heard Brian's voice coming from the basement.

"*Get around the back!*" I heard him holler. It took me a minute to rule out the possibility that I'd imagined it, but then I set the milk carton down on the counter and tiptoed to the top of the stairs.

"*Hurry up, hurry up!*" His voice carried urgently up from the basement. "*Go ... go ... go ... go!*"

"Bri?" I called uncertainly. "Everything okay?"

When he didn't answer, I flicked on the basement stairway light and started down. Downstairs, Brian was nowhere in sight, but his bedroom door was ajar and the room beyond it was dark. I made my way down the hall toward it, not sure why I was tiptoeing.

My brother was a dark, shapeless lump under the bed-covers. "*We're at checkpoint 343, how copy?... watch to your right... hold on, hold on, I can't see through the dust,*" he muttered, twitching and jerking in his sleep. "*Look out, bro, I've got this one... whooooo... ten-four brother, that's a motherfucking hit.*"

I watched him for a while longer, but he didn't say anything more. Gradually, his movements quieted and eventually he appeared to have settled back into sleep. I crept back upstairs, put the milk away, and went back to bed. Watching my sleeping brother back in Afghanistan, shouting frantic communications to his fellow soldiers, had killed my cereal craving.

Too many things about Brian are making me feel unsettled lately: the restlessness he can't shake, his pre-occupation with war updates and with disturbing, violent movies, and also the way I've heard him pick irritably at Victoria until she leaves, crying. Not to mention the empty vodka bottles I've seen in the trash can when I take out the garbage.

The clock beside my bed says two o'clock before I finally drift off into my own troubled sleep.

Mix Tape Ideas for Brian

"Into the Dark" by The Juliana Theory
"Walking on Glass" by The Movielife
"Misery Business" by Paramore
"All Hail the Heartbreaker" by Spill Canvas
"No Place Feels Like Home" by Midtown
"Morale is Low" by Jejune
"Nothing Feels Good" by The Promise Ring
"Buried Myself Alive" by The Used
"The Recluse" by Cursive
"One-Armed Scissor" by At the Drive-In
"In Circles" by Sunny Day Real Estate
"The Suffering" by Coheed and Cambria
"I'm Not Okay (I Promise)" by My Chemical Romance

TWENTY-FOUR

....

While Brian rides the Disoriented Express, Leo's hunger strike continues. I'm so distracted by all there is to worry about that when Ms. Twohey announces we're going to start a project involving self-portraits, I can barely follow her explanation. It's like one of those Charlie Brown television specials: when Twohey says, "It can be anything you want it to be, as long as you choose a medium we've studied this semester," all I hear is *mwhmp-rhmpwhmp, mrphmp-bmrmph-phmp*.

"I don't get it," I whisper to Miranda, who's already sketching.

Miranda barely glances up. "Self-portrait, Dov. What do you *think* she means?"

"That's it?"

"It's supposed to be something that represents you as an artist. A self-portrait from your unique artistic perspective."

Everyone seems to be talking gibberish today. Rather than try to decipher it all, I decide to ask Ms. Twohey if I can go to the library. "I want to do some, uh, research. For my project."

That's what I love about Ms. Twohey: rather than ask what kind of research might possibly be necessary to draw a portrait of myself, she reaches for her pad of hall passes. "I hope you can find something to inspire you," she says with a smile, holding out a pass. I'm reminded that, up close like this, Ms. Twohey is a pretty blinding work of art herself.

"Thanks," I reply sweetly. "Having you as a teacher is usually inspiring enough."

On the way out of class, I grin at Miranda, who mimes puking into her pencil case.

Scarlett was right: there are plenty of gecko sites on the web, and many of them have postings from owners with finicky eaters like Leo. More than one noted that geckos sometimes eat less during the shorter days of fall and winter; kind of like a mini-hibernation period. If this is the problem, things should revert to normal within a month or so. Still, in all the years I've had him, Leo has never gone through something like this before, so I don't put it high on the list of likely possibilities.

Environmental temperature changes are apparently also a common cause of geckos going off their feed. I make a mental note to check the thermometer in Leo's aquarium when I get home, but I'm pretty sure it's holding steady at a balmy 88 degrees. I also plan to double-check the under-tank heater to make sure it's heating uniformly, but I doubt that's the problem.

Another possibility is that Leo is stressed out by something else that's changed in his surroundings. I remember guiltily that I rearranged things the last time I cleaned his aquarium; I hope I haven't inadvertently sent Leo spiraling into anorexia. Still, he doesn't *seem* agitated or disoriented ... if anything, he seems lethargic and *too* calm.

The last, and most concerning possibility, is that Leo has accidentally eaten some of the substrate that covers the bottom of his cage. This, I read on GeckoWorld.com, could cause impaction, a condition which is "potentially fatal." I don't want to think about that possibility.

On the reassuring side, everything I read emphasizes that geckos can survive for weeks on little or no food. I try to remember exactly how long it's been since Leo has eaten normally; to my best recollection, things changed shortly before Brian arrived home. Which means it's going on a month. If things don't resolve soon, there's cause to get seriously worried.

As I'm turning this over in my mind, the pink rectangle of an eraser flies over the top of the computer's monitor and lands with a thud in my lap. Craning my head to the side, I'm surprised to see Koby sitting at a table near the newspapers.

I log off and head across the room. "Hey," I say. "What's up?"

"Sub in math class," Koby says. "I asked if I could come down here and do homework." That's a laugh; anyone who knows Koby knows that he's never done a page of homework in his life. "What are you doing here? Don't you have Twohey right now?" All my friends know that under most circumstances, I'd never miss a minute in Ms. Twohey's radiant presence.

"Leo's not eating," I tell him. "I'm trying to figure out why."

Koby makes a face; all my friends know what Leo means to me. "That sucks."

"I know."

"Listen," Koby says, changing the subject. "What are you doing after school?"

I consider. "Nothing that I know of," I say finally.

Koby waves at the librarian, who's frowning in our direction. "It's my shrink's birthday tomorrow. I want to get him a CD."

I've never heard of anybody buying their shrink a birthday present, but then I've never had a shrink. Maybe it's the normal thing to do. "He says he wants to know more about the kind of music I listen to," Koby adds.

Ah, now it makes sense. Koby's shrink is trying to pry a little deeper into my friend's psyche.

"Ali and I are going to the Dusty Groove; you should come along."

"Sure," I agree. "Let's do it."

Koby thinks he can get his mom's Buick, so we agree they'll pick me up at my house. I'm relieved at the idea of spending a couple hours hanging out with my buddies; it sounds like a great way to take my mind off everything in my life that I can't fix right now.

After school, I drive home and find the Buick already parked by the curb in front of our house. I pull the Gator into the driveway and get out, motioning to the guys that I just need to drop my stuff in the house and I'll be ready to go.

Unfortunately, when I walk in the house, Brian is waiting for me. "I need you to take me downtown," he says, getting up from Dad's chair where he's been waiting. "Victoria's pissed at me again. I want to pick up some flowers before I see her tonight."

"Can't Mom take you?" I ask, glancing out the window to where Koby and Ali are waiting.

"She's not home from work yet," Brian says. "I don't want to wait that long." He's already reaching for his jacket, restless and impatient as usual.

"Maybe you can drive yourself," I suggest. "The Gator's out in the driveway."

"I haven't been cleared to drive yet," he snaps back. Even though his cast has been removed, Brian's doctors are concerned about his depth perception.

I watch him struggle to get his jacket on, knowing he'll shrug me off if I try to help. "The thing is, bro, I already have plans. The guys and I are stopping by the Dusty Groove, and then we'll probably ... "

Brian doesn't miss a beat. "Perfect," he says. "You'll be driving right past the flower shop."

I give up. "I guess."

Now Brian is inviting himself along when I see my friends. I'm irritated, although I try not to show it. I'm glad that neither Koby nor Ali looks all that surprised to see Brian trailing behind me toward the car.

Instead of climbing in back with me, Brian pulls open the Buick's passenger door. "Hey, dude," he says to Ali, "mind if I ride shotgun?"

Ali hesitates, more out of surprise than any kind of actual objection. "I guess," he agrees finally. Still, he shoots me a puzzled look as he climbs in back with me. I shrug to let him know I don't understand what goes on in Brian's head any more than he does.

Brian settles into his seat and locks the Buick's door, which seems unnecessary, since downtown Longview isn't exactly Central LA.

Koby turns up the music and pulls the Buick away from the curb. "So, I'll bet you saw a lot of crazy shit over there, huh?" Koby asks Brian.

"Some," Brian agrees. He's staring out the window, concentrating on the road. I know he's looking for potholes; there's something about them that makes him nervous. Fortunately, the Longview city workers keep the roads of our town in good condition, so we don't encounter any serious threats on the way downtown. I expect Brian to insist that we stop so he can buy the flowers, but he doesn't bring it up, and the next thing I know we're pulling up in front of the Dusty Groove, our favorite Longview music store. We pile out of the Buick and go inside, first Koby, then Ali, then me, with Brian bringing up the rear.

The Dusty Groove is everything you could want in

a music store; the usual array of new and used CDs, cassettes, and vinyl, plus T-shirts and posters, vintage comic books, and a glass case of jewelry for body modification addicts. The place always smells like some type of incense that makes the inside of my nose itch.

"Need help finding anything?" the kid behind the counter asks as we walk in.

"I'm looking for something by Marilyn Manson or maybe some Ozzy Osbourne," Koby replies. The clerk nods and gestures for Koby to follow him.

"What kind of shrink is he seeing, anyway?" Ali mutters as they head off.

I shrug. "A regular one, as far as I know. My guess is that Koby's probably trying to freak him out."

Ali nods thoughtfully. "Probably right."

Brian is over in the vinyl section, flipping through the selections; I watch as he pull an album by Metallica out of the rack and turns it over to study the playlist on the back. In my experience, Brian has never been a big heavy metal fan, but I figure maybe he's looking to expand his collection—perhaps to compliment his newfound love of slasher flicks.

"So, if you had to guess, which of these would you say has the most explicit language?" Koby's asking the clerk, holding up a CD in each hand.

The kid considers. "Well, you can't go wrong with the Manson, but there's always Cypress Hill..."

"Uh-huh. Uh-huh."

I'm just turning around, to tell Ali that Koby's shrink is going to come up with a whole new treatment plan based on his birthday present, when a movement by Brian catches my eye. My heart rate quickens as I realize that, in one swift motion, my brother has pressed an LP against the front of his body and zipped up his jacket to conceal it. He turns and begins walking casually toward me, his face expressionless.

"What are you *doing*?" I hiss. My mouth has gone so dry I can barely get the words out.

"I'll wait for you guys outside," Brian says, ignoring my question. I hold my breath, anticipating the shrill screech of alarms as Brian passes through the security zone, but remarkably, none come. The only sound is the bell of the Dusty Groove's front door swinging closed behind him. Apparently no one is going to notice that my brother has just committed an obvious crime.

"Goddamnit," I mutter to Ali, who looks at me blankly. "I'll be right back."

Outside, Brian is leaning against the Dusty Groove's storefront, scanning the street and sidewalk. "See any suspicious activity?" I ask. "Aside from your own?"

Brian's expression remains neutral. "Nope. All clear."

"So," I ask, "you're a shoplifter now?"

Brian chuckles. "Why do you say that?"

I reach over and pull down the zipper on the front of his jacket, revealing the album behind it. "*That's* why I say that."

Without missing a beat, Brian reaches up and unzips his jacket the rest of the way, letting the album, *Altars of Madness* by Morbid Angel, into view. "Seriously, what does it matter?" he asks me. "It's not like it's important."

"Not to you, maybe," I tell him. "But I'm sure the owners

of the record shop prefer people paying for their merchandise."

Brian shrugs. "Take it back, then," he offers, holding the album out to me.

"Why'd you take it in the first place?" I don't have a lot of money myself, but I know my brother has plenty.

"Dov," Brian says wearily, "chillax. Seriously, it's not worth it, dude. I'm here to tell you that none of this matters. There are so many terrible things going on the world, so much pure evil … it's truly pathetic to even worry about something like this."

When Brian starts talking like this, there's no point in arguing, and I'm halfway relieved when the door of the Dusty Groove swings open and my friends emerge.

"Got it," Koby says brightly, holding up a plastic bag. "He's going to think I'm a psychopath for sure."

"Copy that," Brian says. "Let's roll."

In the car, my brother is suddenly in high spirits, joking and laughing with my friends. He breaks the news about needing to stop at the flower shop, and Koby and Ali cheerfully agree, happy to go anywhere as long as they can remain in the company of the great and powerful Brian Howard. For a few minutes, anyway, my brother seems back on his game, charming my friends with his dynamic personality. Listening to him banter, I can almost be convinced that I imagined the emptiness in his eyes as he stared back at me outside the Dusty Groove.

Almost.

LONGVIEW HERALD
Legendary Local Athlete Arrested

Well-known Longview High athlete and National Guard hero, Brian Howard, 20, is charged with theft after being apprehended Saturday following a report of theft from an area music store.

When contacted for comment, the owner of the Dusty Groove expressed shock, stating, "We might have expected this from his brother (Dov Howard, 16), but never from Brian. I'm still thinking this entire thing must be a terrible mistake."

Authorities are investigating any possible involvement by Dov Howard…

TWENTY-FIVE

(CNN)—Military officials confirmed today that the most dangerous threat for U.S. troops in Afghanistan comes from an unexpected source: roadside bombs. These bombs, often referred to as IEDs or "improvised explosive devices," are responsible for 70-80 percent of casualties, according to Admiral Mike Mullen, chairman of the Joint Chiefs of Staff...

....

Too soon, the weekend of our much-anticipated hunting trip is upon me. "There's got to be a way I can get out of this nightmare," I moan to Leo.

'Fraid not, Grasshopper. Your ticket says round trip on this one.

Just when I think things can't get any worse, Dad comes off the road early and insists we have to leave for the hunting shack on Friday night rather than early on Saturday morning, as originally planned. "It'll give us a chance to get up and do some scouting before dawn," Dad tells me, obviously pleased.

Before dawn? This is just getting better and better.

With Brian's arm just out of the sling, it's all on me when it comes to helping Dad load up the Suburban for the trip. "Helping Dad" mostly involves Dad supervising and criticizing me as I haul sleeping bags, camping supplies, boxes of food and ammo, and the rifles in their canvas covers. To my relief, we're only bringing two guns, one for Dad and one for Brian. I have zero interest in being schooled in the most efficient methods of killing.

"All right... that oughtta do it," Dad finally decrees, giving everything one last once-over.

"Are you sure?" I ask, exhausted. "What about the kitchen sink? That's still in the house."

No comment from Dad, who is now looking *me* over. "You got some clothes to bring?" he asks. "What I mean is, you're not planning on going out in that kind of a getup, are you?"

I glance down. Without even being reminded, I'd pulled on a faded old pair of Levi's I'd found buried deep in the back of my closet. Besides that, I'm wearing a MCR T-shirt, a yellow hoodie, and tennis shoes, none of which seemed likely to provoke my father.

"Um..." I say cautiously, "what's wrong with this?" It's a loaded question, but I decide that in honor of our hunting trip, I might as well pull the trigger.

Dad sighs impatiently. "Well, first of all," he says, "your feet will freeze in those flimsy things. You need some boots . . . some of your brother's old ones, maybe. Ask your mother; she knows where all that stuff is."

"Okay."

"And I'm betting those are the same clothes you wore to school today."

"Not all of them," I mumble. Even he should know I wouldn't be caught dead in these jeans.

"To a deer, you're going to smell like books and gym shoes and whatever else school smells like these days. Nothing that a deer is used to smelling, I'll tell ya that. Why do you think your mother washes our hunting clothes in unscented detergent?"

Apparently I missed the memo about Mom's role in the plot to kill Bambi. Frankly, however, nothing could surprise me at this point.

It doesn't matter; Dad is on a roll. "And listen, that whole getup will reflect the light like a neon sign."

This whole thing is getting downright silly, if you ask me. "What do you *want* me to wear, then?" I demand. "It's not like I have a closet full of wool and camo."

Dad gives me a look that says my tone is tiptoeing awfully close to the line of disrespect, but I just stare defiantly back at him. After all, what's he going to do . . . *make me stay home?*

Instead, he narrows his eyes in a glare designed to intimidate. "Go see if your mother has finished packing the cooler," he barks. I've pushed things farther than was comfortable for either of us, so I turn obediently and trot back toward the house. Behind me, I can hear Dad muttering angrily to himself.

It's nearly an hour later when we finally pull out of the driveway. Dad is in the driver's seat and Brian is in the passenger seat. I, of course, ride in the back, squeezed in between gear and supplies.

The sun is sinking low on the horizon and Dad is disappointed we've gotten such a late start. "It'll be pitch black by the time we get there," he grumbles. "I was hoping we could get a look around tonight yet, see if there are any signs of bedding."

"Don't worry, Dad," Brian says. "It'll be dark, but we can send Dov out with a flashlight."

I reach over the seat and smack the back of his head. "Very funny." The last thing I need is for Dad to decide that's a great idea. Anyway, I wouldn't even know what I was looking for. "What does that mean, anyway?"

Dad puts on the pickup's blinker to turn onto the highway. "Scouting for bedding sites," he tells me. "Bucks spend the whole night chasing down doe, then they bed down before daybreak. Right around midday … when they're all rested up … that's when we want to be ready for them. He positions one arm as if he has a rifle pressed to his shoulder. "That way they're staggering around, still half asleep, and … ka-blam!" He shoots Brian an appreciative grin. "I imagine you'll show me up good this year, what with all the target practice you've had lately."

I watch for my brother's reaction, but when he speaks, his voice is steady. "No doubt," he says. "I can't wait to get my hands back on a firearm. There's something so sooth-ing about firing a weapon."

Man, I'm going to get *all* the girls with a sweet line like that.

The hunting shack is located in godforsaken country about an hour north of Longview; from what I under-stand, Dad and Brian rent the same cabin every fall. By the time the Suburban turns off the highway and crunches onto gravel, the blackening sky is brightened to navy by the moon overhead. It rained earlier in the week, and the Suburban's tires bump and skitter across the washboard surface of the road, sending our high beams bouncing cra-zily. Before I know it, we're pulling up in front of a run-down structure—it's the legendary "hunting shack." With an emphasis on *shack*.

"I'll head inside and get some light going," Dad informs us as he shuts off the engine. "You boys can start unloading."

Brian opens the passenger door and jumps out, his heels crunching in the gravel as I reach across the sleep-ing bags and spring my own door handle. First things first: nature is calling.

Once I've relieved myself into some scrub bushes, I come back, expecting to find Brian making a pile of things for me to carry inside. He's nowhere to be seen; the only movement is from inside the cabin, where a blaze of light tells me Dad is making progress. A moment later, Dad crosses in front of one of the grimy windows, a kerosene lantern in his hand. The conditions are even worse than I imagined; I can hardly *wait* to see where I'll be sleeping.

"Brian?" I call. When there's no answer, I glance around nervously, hoping my brother isn't going to start the weekend off by scaring the shit out of me. It's just my luck he'll do something to send me screaming toward the cabin like a girl. I'll have to listen to Dad and Brian giving me crap about it for the rest of the weekend.

"Brian?" I call again, steeling myself against any sudden attacks. "Bri?"

"*Keep it down*," Brian whispers sharply from directly behind me.

Wheeling around, I find Brian standing behind me, his back inches from mine. Even though I tried to prepare myself, it's a good thing I've already emptied my bladder. "Jesus, Brian!" I snap, "Don't sneak up on me like that. Where were you, anyway?"

Brian turns toward me. "Checking the perimeter," he mutters. "All clear." In the light of the moon, his eyes are unnaturally bright; for some reason, Edward Cullen crosses my mind, and I curse the day Miranda made me watch *Twilight*.

"Knock it off, dude. And don't tell me to keep it down," I add irritably. "We're out in the middle of nowhere." I rub my arms, pretending that the reason I'm shivering is because it's cold.

"You're right about that," Brian agrees cryptically.

"Whatever that means," I retort, avoiding looking at him. We've only just arrived and already I'm wishing this little vacation was over.

Somewhere along the line, Brian already unloaded his

rifle from the Suburban; now he picks it up and threads the straps of his duffel bag over his shoulder. I watch him double-check to make sure the Suburban's doors are locked, which seems ridiculous considering we're miles from civilization. "Grab the other stuff," he instructs me, staggering a little as he heads toward the shack.

"Roger-wilco." I salute. *Oh yeah*, I think bitterly as I load my arms with gear, *this is gonna be LOADS of fun.*

NARRATOR: *"You are traveling through another dimension, a dimension not only of sight and sound, but of mind. A journey into a wondrous land of both shadow and substance, a land of imagination. Next stop … the Twilight Zone…"*

TWENTY-SIX

Inside the hunting shack, the woodstove is having a hard time overcoming the cold November air. Soon I'm shivering, despite having pulled on the extra sweatshirt Mom forced me to bring. The rest of my hunting party doesn't seem a bit bothered by the cold; Brian even shed his jacket. He's sitting on a battered kitchen chair, oiling his gun with a soft white rag.

"You boys as hungry as I am?" Dad asks jovially. He's lit the gas stove, and I watch as he pours several cans of beans into a pot from a cupboard over the sink. I hope he's wiped it out, at least. Dad locates the package of brats Mom packed, then slices them into the beans. A few minutes later I'm encouraged to find that even though I'm slowly turning into the abominable snowman version of myself, the food smells great.

Dad looks up from the stove. "What … you cold, Dov?"

"Are you kidding me? You can see your breath in here."

"Don't be a … " I watch as Dad catches himself. I know Mom's voice is scolding in his head: *You don't give Dov a hard time now, you hear me, Mick?* He sighs, then finishes with, "It'll warm up in here in a minute."

I'm just thinking *wow, Dad's kind of trying*, when he drops the spoon in the beans and strides the few steps to where I'm curled, kittenlike, on the threadbare sofa. His rough fingers brush my neck as he pulls my T-shirt away from my throat, peering inside. "No *wonder* you're cold, kid," he scoffs. "You're not wearing any long johns."

Brian glances up from his work. "No long johns?" he repeats absently. "There's an extra pair in my duffel, bro."

Disgusted, Dad releases my T-shirt and goes back to the beans as I reluctantly unfold myself and go to find Brian's duffel. He's set it just inside the only other room, a rough-walled bedroom furnished with two rickety sets of bunks. As I kneel and unzip Brian's bag, an icy draft comes from the direction of the window; something tells me that even inside my sleeping bag, it's going to be a long, frigid night.

Mom sealed most of Brian's hunting clothes into plastic bags, presumably to keep them from being contaminated by the nasty scent of anything human. I locate the package containing the extra set of long underwear and undo the stay-fresh seal, letting the thin, waffled fabric unfurl into my lap. It's hard to imagine how this flimsy layer of cloth is going to make me feel any warmer.

As I stuff the empty plastic bag back into the duffel,

my hand brushes against something solid. Without thinking, I pull it out of the duffel into the moonlight shining through the window... then nearly drop it when I realize it's a revolver.

"Hey," I call. "What's up with this, Brian?"

"With what?" A minute later, my brother appears in the doorway. His jaw tenses when he sees me holding the gun. "Oh," he says. "It's a firearm, moron."

"Uh...yeah, that part I get." I lay the gun carefully back in the bottom of the bag, hoping it isn't loaded. There are many questions to be asked, but I can't put any of them into words.

"You find the long johns?"

"Yeah." I shiver, trying not to think about the fact that I have to undress in order to put them on. At least there will be no problem fitting them under the butt-ugly baggy Levis.

Peeling clothes off in the chill of the bedroom is painful, but worth it; once I manage to scramble into the long johns and back into my clothes, I begin to feel better almost immediately. It isn't clear whether it's the extra layer of clothing or the fact that the wood stove has finally coughed forth enough warmth to heat the shack, but either way, I'm able to relax enough to eat my share of brats and beans.

"*BLLRRRRPPPP!*" Brian lets loose one of his famous deep belches. "Good chow, Dad." He's right—the food is delicious and did its job warming me up from the inside. Now that I'm feeling better, sleep seems like more of a possibility.

"Yup," Dad agrees, patting his stomach. "Good stuff."

After we finish, he collects our paper plates, stuffing

them both deep into the plastic garbage bag he's brought along. The shack doesn't have running water, so the best Dad can do is rinse off our utensils in a bit of drinking water and wipe out the cooking pot with a handful of paper towels.

As he ties the garbage bag closed, Dad watches Brian, who's stretching his shoulder carefully. "You sure you're going to be able to manage the rifle tomorrow, buddy?" he asks. "That kick might be a little rough on the shoulder."

"I'm not worried," Brian says. "It's just a little stiff yet. At night, mostly."

Dad clears his throat. "You haven't told us about it yet," he says. "What exactly happened over there? Your injuries, I mean."

I'm surprised to see Dad asking so gently; I've never known him to be shy, or even careful, when asking about something he wants to know.

My brother glances at me, as if hoping I'll assure him it's all right not to talk about it. I don't say anything; I admit that, like Dad, I'm curious too.

"Well," Brian begins slowly, then stops and clears his throat. He continues haltingly. "It was kind of a fluke, actually. My unit was walking security patrol on the fringes of Kabul. We'd gotten some intell about an insurgency hideout, but when we got there it was our worst nightmare; a residential neighborhood with a million places to hide. Worst of all, in a setting like that there's a pretty good potential for collateral damage, if you know what I'm saying."

I don't. "Collateral damage?"

Brian coughs dryly. "Civilians accidentally get hurt."

Ah, now I understand: "collateral damage" means "killing innocent people that get in the way."

Brian continues. "The insurgents must have gotten some intell of their own, because from the minute we showed up, we were getting hit with sniper fire. It was pretty nuts; rounds were pinging off of buildings and basically just hailing down all around us. We got a bead on where it was coming from and got our own sniper in position. Then we launched a mortar that pretty much wiped out the building where we figured they were hiding."

"Nice," Dad inserts, his tone admiring.

"There was a little lull in the action so we were able to advance. We were the force on the street, but the Bradleys were following along behind, backing us up."

Listening to Brian, I can picture the scene as clearly as if I was watching it myself. Dust and debris floating in the air from the mortar explosive, Brian and the rest of his unit tense and shouting as they advance, their ears ringing from the din of artillery.

Brian has a faraway look, as if the whole scene is happening in front of his eyes too. "We set up temporary headquarters in an empty house. There were verses from the Koran written on the doorways and a painting of Mecca on the wall in the front room. Insurgents had clearly been there; there were dirty blankets on the floor, rotted food and garbage everywhere. Someone had taken a reeking shit in the stairwell. The whole thing got pretty intense; we knew there were more of them, but they were staying one step ahead of us. It was really pissing us off. Occasionally our sniper would get one and the body would be left lying in the street. After the sun went down, cats and dogs would eat on them."

"Gah," Dad says. Even he looks a little green in the flickering light of the lantern.

"So, by the second day of this, we were pretty shot. Someone radioed that they'd seen suspicious activity in a house up the way, so we headed over there. One of my buddies shot the door up and another guy started kicking it in. I was near the back of the pack while this was going on, and as we were heading in, all of the sudden I noticed this jumble of wires off to the side of the house. Something about these wires didn't seem right, so I detoured over to check it out. And I find out that the wires are connected to a propane tank."

"Rigged-up explosive," Dad breathes.

Brian nods. "My thoughts exactly. I figure they're trying to get us all in position and then, KABLAM. So I grab for my radio, and then … all of the sudden, the whole thing explodes."

I stop breathing. "The propane tank?" This must have been how Brian was injured.

"No," Brian says, reaching up to run a shaky hand through his hair. "The building. It was a set-up, but not the kind I thought. There weren't a bunch of insurgents inside the house—there was only one. He'd wired himself with a bomb and detonated it once my unit was in range."

"Jesus," Dad says.

"If you'd gone in, you would have been killed along with everyone else," I whisper.

My brother gives me a look I can't read. "So, I caught some shrapnel in my eye and got hit with flying debris. My shoulder and ribs got nailed with something big, and something else hit me in the head, or maybe it was just the blast... I don't know what happened, really, because I don't remember anything after that. Blast concussion, they call it."

"Everyone else was killed," I murmur.

Brian nods. "Yeah," he says hoarsely. "All of them. I was the only one who made it back to the safe house, and I don't even remember how I got there. It's amazing I wasn't picked off; anyone could have easily taken me out. And to be totally honest, part of me wished it had happened like that."

Neither Dad nor I know what to say to that. Chance, guardian angel, Brian's usual luck... there's no real sense to be made of what happened.

An invisible draft makes the lantern light waver; in it, I catch sight of Dad, whose face looks several years older than it did when Brian started his tale.

"I guess it just wasn't your time," Dad says finally.

"Wasn't it?" Brian retorts, looking levelly at Dad. "And why not?"

Dad hesitates. I expect him to say something that will make it all make sense, but instead he shakes his head and pushes back his chair. "That's quite a story," is all he says. "Quite a story." Dad clears his throat. "Well, it looks like we're almost out of fuel, boys. Probably a good time to hit the hay."

And that's it. Without further discussion, we go to bed. It seems a little bizarre to me; Brian has just told us a terrible story … not just a story, but something that had actually happened to him … and now the three of us are all acting like we haven't heard it. I don't know what to make of it.

By unspoken default, I get the top bunk. I climb up gingerly, feeling the rickety structure tremble and shake beneath me with every movement I make. Once I'm satisfied that the mattress is going to hold my weight and not send me crashing down on top of Brian, I crawl into the cold nylon sleeping bag and zip it up to my chin. Dad puts out the lamp and uses the moonlight from the window to find his way to the other bunk across the room; it isn't long before his snores begin to rumble through the silence. I imagine his feet twitching like a dog's, deep inside his sleeping bag, as he dreams of tramping through the fields and trees, looking for things to kill.

I'm still wound up from everything Brian said and think at first that I won't be able to sleep, but the sleeping bag contains my warmth and it isn't long before my eyes began to grow heavy. I roll onto my side and am almost asleep when the bed begins to shake with movement from below, bringing me swimming back to consciousness.

I open my eyes a slit and watch as Brian emerges from beneath and stands up. As he creeps away slowly in the darkness, I lift my head to get a better view. My brother is rummaging around in his duffel, and the minute he withdraws his hand, I don't need the light from the window to know what it is he was searching for.

As if I'm holding it myself, I imagine how the pistol feels in Brian's hand—the cool, deadly heft of it. I know the weapon means something completely different to each of us: to me it's an object of danger, but to my brother, it's just the opposite.

I endure more bunk-bed jitterbugging as Brian crawls back into bed. A few minutes later, my brother's snores are playing a duet with Dad's. I wait as long as I can, then gingerly reposition myself, through a series of tentative maneuvers, until I can hang my head over the bunk's edge.

Brian lies snoring in the bunk below, the gun clasped securely against his chest, asleep... but on constant alert against anything terrible that might come for him in the night.

TWENTY-SEVEN

....

When Brian nudges me roughly awake the next morning, the sky outside the window is still waiting for a phone call from dawn. The wood stove in the other room must have burned down low, because my brother's frosty breath makes him look like a smoke-breathing dragon. "Get 'er moving, Dov," he says. "Time to do our part to reduce the deer population."

When I finally manage to make it out to the main room, blinking blearily, Dad is already gone. Brian is sitting up on the couch, pulling on his boots.

"Aren't we going to have breakfast?" I complain, even though I often don't eat in the morning. It's simply a way to forestall the inevitable.

"You bet." Brian tosses me a couple granola bars. Since my hands are cowering deep inside my pockets, "breakfast" hits me in the chest and falls to the floor at my feet.

"Great," I mutter. I sink onto the couch beside him. "I seriously don't think I can do this."

"Don't be a baby."

"Sorry, *Dad*."

Brian reaches for a pair of coveralls and tosses them toward me. "Put these on over your clothes. Dad brought in another jacket for you from the truck."

He watches, grinning and impatient, as I struggle into them. It occurs to me that I'm not going to get any sympathy from my brother. He *loves* this.

"Ready to go catch up with Dad?"

"No." Nevertheless, I follow Brian outside into the frigid air. "Cheese and rice," I gasp. "Balls."

"It'll make a man out of ya," Brian laughs. He takes in a lungful of frost-sharpened air. "Damn, I missed this!"

There's nothing to do but get the show on the road. Loaded under backpacks containing what I presume is lunch, we head out, my brother carrying the rifle loosely in his right hand with the business end pointed toward the ground.

Despite the frigid temperatures, the sky is clear and painting itself with pink and purple streaks as the sun throws a leg up over the horizon. We walk along briskly, pushing white puffs of our breath into the air ahead of us. The grass is rigid with early morning frost, and makes a satisfying crunching sound as we crush it under our feet.

Brian glances sideways and catches me almost smiling. "It's great to be out here, right?" he demands. "Come on, admit it."

"Whatever."

My brother chuckles. "You know what?" he says, looking around. "This kinda reminds me of being over there."

I glance around at the flat brown landscape broken only by tall Minnesota pines. "Seriously?" I can't imagine how this landscape could bear any similarity to Afghanistan.

"Of course, the terrain looks different. And it sure as hell *smells* different."

"Yeah," I say, like I know what he means.

"I guess it's just the part about walking along like this, looking for … you know. Just looking for stuff. Except now we're not the ones in danger. Sure glad about that."

"Mm-hmm." I wonder if we should be talking so much. Aren't we supposed to be quiet so as not to scare away any deer?

Brian's tone turns philosophical. "You know," he says thoughtfully, "once you've been there awhile, everything starts to feel different. I mean, of course you're scared, but it's not that. It's more like … like you're living right at the edge of something. Your senses … the way you hear things and the way you see things and … it's just all turned up to the highest level. You'd think it would be terrible, painful even, but it's just the opposite, Dov. Everything is so *real*. Realer than real. It's like you're … awake, really awake and paying attention for the first time. Man, before I went over, I *thought* I was alive, but really, I wasn't even out of the packaging yet."

I nod, and in a way I do understand. I get that you can just drift along, letting life wash harmlessly over you; it's a way of making sure nothing penetrates deep enough to hurt. My friends and I have mastered the art of living this way; I never suspected that my brother has too.

"I remember this one day," Brian continues. "We were sent to check out this shelled-out village. We were looking for whatever... unexploded IEDs, people who needed help, whatever. There was nothing, though: everything was just decimated. Everywhere you looked, there was nothing but rubble. People's homes ruined, their lives destroyed... for some reason, it was like the most beautiful thing I'd ever seen. Weird, huh?"

I nod. We agree on that, anyway.

"Even though I *was* scared over there," Brian admits, "somehow it was also the best... the best thing I've ever done. I just kept thinking, 'Man, this is life. Finally... *life*.'"

We tramp along, both of us thinking. I steal a glance sideways at my brother, the familiar line of his shoulders, the sharp cut of his jaw against the lightening sky. "At least you're safe here," I say finally.

"True dat, bro," Brian sighs. "True dat."

If I'm not mistaken, there's something in his voice that sounds an awful lot like regret.

TWENTY-EIGHT

(NPR)—Last month's suicide toll among U.S. soldiers rose to 24, the highest monthly total since the Army began compiling statistics in 1980, and more than the number of deaths sustained in the same month by all other branches of the armed forces combined. Gen. Peter Chiarelli, vice chief of staff of the Army, told NPR's Robert Johnson that the Army is actively researching the issue in an attempt to learn why suicide numbers continue to rise.

....

We tramp along for another mile or two as the frost burns off and the sun rises higher in the sky. I have no idea how Brian knows where we'll find Dad, but he seems to be responding to some kind of internal GPS. We see no deer, although at one point a beaver scurries across our paths. It pauses to consider, regarding us with no real concern. "Don't shoot him," I whisper worriedly to Brian. I have no idea about the rules of hunting: perhaps anything that moves is fair game. I'm relieved when Brian chuckles. "Don't be a moron," he tells me. The beaver shakes its head as if it, too, is disappointed in me, then ambles off on its way, no worse the wear for having encountered a pair of baboons.

Hiking over uneven ground in Dad's heavy boots is starting to make my feet hurt. I think about complaining, but Brian seems lost in thought, his eyes studying the horizon. I begin to wonder whether we might be lost. How far could Dad have gone, anyway?

Just as I'm about to raise the issue, a nearby shot breaks the mid-morning quiet. It sounds like a starting pistol. "Get ready ... get set ... kill!" I quip.

Brian doesn't respond, but he changes our direction, heading us closer to Dad or deer, whichever we find first. "Keep watch," he instructs me, although I'm not sure for what. As we approach a grove of trees, I suddenly see movement and a flash of hunter orange. "Hey." I point. "I think that's Dad over ... "

"DOWN! DOWN! DOWN!" Brian shouts, throwing himself behind a crop of boulders and dragging me down with him.

Bundled up in coveralls and unstable in Dad's oversized boots, I fall awkwardly onto my side and lose my wind for a second. "What the hell are you doing?" I demand when I get my breath back.

Brian ignores me; he's busy talking into his shoulder. "Alpha Company under attack," he jabbers, his tone pitched higher and harsher than usual. "We're on foot and mobile, but they've got us pinned down, Captain—must be three or four belt-fed SOBs. Requesting permission to be cleared for response."

"Brian!" I snap. "Listen to me!"

"Holy fuck, there must be twenty of them, Wilkie," Brian mutters, taking the safety off his rifle.

The seriousness of the situation suddenly begins to dawn on me, just as the sound of movement comes from the trees up ahead. "Wait!" I holler, just as Brian jumps to his feet, points the gun into the trees, and fires.

There's a click but nothing more; as if he doesn't notice, my brother grips his weapon as it jerks and jerks and jerks again, like round after round is firing at an unseen enemy.

I don't know why the rifle jammed, and I don't stop to think about it. Instead, I scramble to my feet and run as fast as I can toward the group of trees, nearly tripping over Dad's boots with every step. "Dad!" I roar. "Get down!"

Behind me, I hear my brother fumbling with the weapon. "Sonuva*bitch*!" he curses to no one I can see. "I'm jammed! You're on your own, Sarg—I can't cover you!"

To my relief, Dad emerges from the trees, seemingly oblivious to the fact that he's in mortal danger. "Stop that hollering," he orders. "You'll scare the deer. I've just found a bedding patch ... where's your brother?"

I look behind me and discover that Brian has disappeared. Nervously, I grab Dad's arm and pull him deeper into the trees, out of range. "Dad," I say urgently, "Brian's having some kind of hallucination."

"Hallucination?" Dad echoes, looking at me but not comprehending.

"It's like he thinks he's in Afghanistan," I manage, looking over my shoulder to the rock formation where I left Brian. He's nowhere to be seen; for all I know, he's circling around to ambush us from behind. "We have to find him and get the gun out of his hands. I'm afraid if he sees us first he might take a shot at us if he doesn't come out of it."

"Take a shot at us?" Dad's turning into a regular parrot. "Your brother would never..." Dad trails off, looking doubtful. Thoughtfully, his eyes follow mine back to the rocks.

"I swear to God, Dad. He's losing it!"

Despite the fact that I'm trying to save his life, Dad glares at me. "Listen kid, if this is some kind of joke you're pulling, you're going to be awfully sorry," he warns.

"No joke, Dad. He just kind of... snapped." I think back to what we were doing, just walking along, listening to the birds and the distant sounds of gunfire...

"We heard shooting," I say, understanding now. "It must have thrown him into some kind of flashback."

I've finally gotten through: Dad looks genuinely worried. "Where is he now?" he asks. "What direction, anyway?"

"I wish I knew."

Dad considers. "Well, we can't just leave him out here running around with a rifle. We've got to track him down."

Trying to look every direction at once, I follow along behind Dad as we head out of the trees in search of my brother, who's probably also hunting for us. We don't have to go far; as we backtrack across the field, I spot Brian sitting on the trunk of a fallen tree, his rifle leaning against his knee. I nudge Dad, my mouth gone dry. "Over there," I manage.

Brian looks up and smiles as we approach, but I still don't trust him. "What if this is some sort of trick?" I whisper to Dad. "You know … like a trap."

Dad lifts a hand to wave. "Brian!" he calls steadily. "We lost you for a bit, buddy. Everything okay?"

Brian nods. "Just waiting on you two," he says.

As we close the distance between us, I study him warily. Nothing about my brother looks unusual.

"Doin' okay, kiddo?" Dad asks, reaching out a hand to pat Brian's knee before dropping down onto the fallen tree beside him.

"No deer yet," Brian complains, as if that's the only thing on his mind. "You see anything?"

"Found a pretty good bedding spot. Want to check it out?"

"Time's a wastin'," Brian agrees. He stands up and grabs his gun. "I'm having a little trouble with the recoil on this thing," he says to Dad, who takes the gun from him and begins to examine it.

My mouth is hanging open; I can't believe it. *Really? Are we really going to act like nothing crazy just happened here?!*

"Wait a minute," I sputter, grabbing Brian by the sleeve of his camo coat. "What about … you were going to take a shot at Dad!" I accuse.

Brian stares at me, his expression blank.

"Don't act like it didn't happen! We heard shooting, and then suddenly you got it in your head that Dad was … I don't know … the *Taliban* … and you pulled me down behind those rocks … " I point, accusing.

Brian reaches up and wipes his hand over his face; for the first time, I notice his forehead is beaded with sweat despite the cool morning air. "Look, bro, I was just messing with you. I mean, *obviously*, right? I didn't expect you to take me seriously."

I stare at him, disbelieving. I know what I saw, and it was real.

Dad laughs. "Well, you scared the hell out of the kid," he tells Brian. "You should have seen his face when he came running up to me. I thought for sure he'd seen Sasquatch."

They chuckle together at my expense, but I notice Brian won't meet my eyes.

After that, there's nothing to do but go on. We fall back into a loose formation with Dad leading the way, then Brian, and finally me; at this point, I'm not going to take my eyes off of anyone.

We cross a small stream, and half a mile later Dad suddenly stops in his tracks. *Over there*, he mouths silently. My eyes follow his signal and I see it standing in a sunny clearing that's visible through some trees on our left: an enormous buck. I have no idea why it hasn't sensed our approach, but now it simply stands there, its proud rack of pronged horns spanning at least four feet on either side of its head.

"*Nice*," Dad whispers.

An instant later, the world explodes.

TWENTY-NINE

....

"Why can't you look me in the eeeyyyye…" my Tranquil Beast ringtone blasts from the pocket of my jacket, where I stowed my phone. The buck alerts, its regal head pivoting smoothly toward us.

"What the… *dammit, Dov*!" Dad explodes.

Before he can finish flipping out at me, another kind of explosion comes from Brian's gun. Ker-BLAM! Dad and I turn in time to see the buck, set to bolt, freeze in mid-air, its head disintegrating in a foamy blur of blood and bone.

"You motherfucker!" Brian shouts. *Click! Click! Click!* He continues firing even though the chamber of his rifle is empty. "Goddamn raghead son-of-a-bitch!"

"Okay!" Dad hollers, grabbing the barrel of Brian's gun and pushing it to the ground. "You got him."

In the aftermath, the air is silent—aside from the pounding of my heart and a high-pitched ringing in my ears. "Guess we won't be mounting this one," Dad observes. He gives Brian a sideways look. Despite the fact that my heart is pounding, part of me is relieved; if this doesn't prove to Dad that *something* isn't right with Brian, I don't know what will convince him.

Brian doesn't respond; his gun is hanging loosely at his side now. "Motherfucking abi-dabis," he mutters under his breath. I shake my head in disbelief; the old Brian was the least racist person I knew.

Dad and I lock eyes, and for the first time in my life I see uncertainty, maybe even fear, in my father's face. Then it's gone, leaving me to wonder if it was only my imagination. "Well, let's get to it," Dad commands, pushing forward through the grass toward the clearing where the dead buck lies.

I follow behind as we head toward the downed animal, fumbling for the pocket on my jacket until I finally manage to pull my phone free. Under *Missed Calls*, I see Ali's name and number listed twice; once from a few minutes ago, and a second time from earlier, around when I'd stepped outside the cabin this morning to relieve myself. Rats; it would be nice to talk to a sane person right about now.

In the clearing, the dark musk of blood and sudden fear hang heavily in the air, clogging my throat and making me feel sick. "What a mess," Dad mutters, standing over the corpse. I hang back, not wanting to get too close. Still, it's impossible not to see the buck's warm brown eye burst from the security of its socket, hanging by a few ragged strands of tissue.

I can't do much more than stare, dry-mouthed, as Dad sets to work with his hunting knife, cutting out the buck's windpipe and working his way down toward the entrails. After a moment, Brian seems to come to his senses, and steps forward to help, bracing and maneuvering the carcass to make things easier for Dad. Together they roll the deer over to let the blood drain; the coppery odor in the air grows heavier as they work. I'm grateful they don't seem to expect anything from me; eventually I wander off, pretending I have to pee, when in fact I'm just trying keep from puking. With my back turned to the scene, I stare up at the sky and notice that Brian was right; the sky does look surreally blue, the trees vivid and sharp-edged against it.

I stay away as long as I can, and when I return, they're nearly finished. I try not to look at the still-steaming pile of entrails, but in the periphery of my vision I can sense the deer's discombobulated eyeball staring at me accusingly from the middle of it all.

"Dov, you'll have to help me carry this monster back to the shack," Dad informs me. He's breathing hard from the exertion of field-dressing the large animal. "Brian's not going to be able to help much, and we'll need to hurry. Skinning is easier while the carcass is still warm."

I nod, dreading the prospect of touching any part of the decimated buck. When I take hold, however, my first thought is of how much coarser the hide is than I expected. While I'm thinking about this, my nostrils are suddenly filled with the rich, primal tang of a wild beast whose only encounter with humans ended in terror, pain, and death. *I'll never forget that smell*, I remember Brian saying. *I couldn't get that smell out of my head for days.*

The trek back to camp under the weight of the buck seems endless, and by the time we arrive my shoulders are aching. Brian is carrying the backpacks and rifles; he seems happy and energized by the kill, and I'm happy that he seems to be back with us in the present.

At the shack, the hollow cavity of the deer is rinsed with water and dried thoroughly with an old towel Dad got from the Suburban. Brian and Dad tie a rope to the buck's hind feet and throw it over a tree branch, which makes it possible for them to hoist the carcass to a hanging position for efficient skinning. I feign interest for a few minutes until I figure it's safe to wander off and call Ali.

It takes a while to find a spot where I have a bar or two of cell phone service, but finally I wedge myself up into an old tree and pick up a signal.

"Hey," Ali answers. I take a deep breath; it's an overwhelming relief to hear his familiar voice. "How's life on the wild side?" he asks.

"Remember when your mom took us to see *Deliverance* during that film festival at the university?"

"Yeah…?"

"It's been kinda like that."

I glance back toward the hunting shack and see Brian beginning to work on skinning the buck; the knife in his hand is already smeared with blood. Even from the tree,

I can see my brother's face: he's crying. A line from the movie comes into my mind: *Night has fallen. And there's nothin' we can do about it.*

"Well, if anyone shows up with a banjo, get the hell out of there," Ali advises.

We finish our conversation and hang up. I think about calling Miranda; I could use one of her dark angels right about now. I'm scrolling for her number when I see Dad on the near side of the shack. "Dov?" he calls, looking for me. There's no choice but to snap the phone shut and climb out of the tree.

I catch up with him on the other side of the shack. "What's up?" I ask. I halfway expect him to snap at me for disappearing, but he doesn't.

"Uh, I've been thinking," Dad says, his eyes somewhere off in the distance. "Maybe we should head back home a little early."

"Seriously?"

Dad glances back toward the shack. "Well, I don't think your brother's doing as well as either of us thought he would," he explains.

You got that right.

"I, uh, I can see his ribs are hurting him, and that shoulder too," he continues. "He's not complaining or anything, but I think he's pretty uncomfortable."

Brian had evidenced no signs of pain that I'd noticed, but then again, I'd been pretty distracted by his craziness. "Sure, if you think we should go. Although I'm kind of bummed that we have to leave early," I add in a sad voice.

Dad turns and looks at me closely; I prepare myself for the forthcoming lecture on being a smart-ass, but it doesn't come. "Listen, Dov," he says instead. "I've been thinking...maybe it would be better to keep some of the things that went on out here just between the three of us. Don't mention it to your mother, is what I'm saying."

Even if Dad wants to keep his head in the sand, I've been counting on the fact that once Mom hears the story of Brian being catapulted back to imaginary Afghanistan, she'll see the importance of getting him some help. "But don't you think..."

"You know how your mother overreacts," Dad interrupts. "She'd blow this thing up into something bigger than it needs to be. Your brother just needs more time. It's like that for every soldier. You'll see."

The look on my face must be doubtful, but Dad reads it differently.

"Don't be so upset about leaving, Dov," he reassures me. "There's always next year. To be honest, I didn't think you'd enjoy hunting so much. I don't know why I never thought to bring you along before."

Not replying is the best response I can manage.

Brian doesn't argue when Dad proposes heading home. He mutters something about needing to spend some time with Victoria anyway, then helps load up the Suburban. I notice he even carries his own duffel out to the truck; when I think of the pistol buried deep down inside it, I decide not to argue. Dad wraps what's left of the buck loosely in a plastic sheet and tosses it up on the roof rack, tying the whole thing down with twine.

A half hour later we pull back onto the highway toward home. I open my phone to text, but discover the battery has run out of charge. I'll have to wait until we get back.

Fortunately, a day spent walking for miles in the crisp, fresh air has tired me out, and before I know it I fall asleep, my head resting against a rolled sleeping bag. When I awake to Dad and Brian arguing in the front, I open my eyes only a slit.

"I'm *not* trying to tell you what to do," Dad snaps. "I'm just saying, sometimes it's hard for me to understand where your head is at these days."

"I don't *expect* you to understand," Brian retorts. "Unless you've been over there, you can't understand how it gets in your blood. Sometimes I feel like ... " He trails off, thinking before he finishes. "Like a part of me got left over there. Like I'm not whole anymore."

Dad's shaking his head, frustrated. "It's going to kill your mother if you tell her you want to go back, you know," he fumes. "Not to mention Victoria. She's putting together a wedding. She thinks you're getting married, Brian. You asked her to marry you!"

"I know." Brian sighs. "I know. I'm just ... not sure that's such a good idea anymore. Not right now, anyway."

Through my eyelashes, I watch Dad's head snap around toward Brian. "You gonna throw that away too now?" he barks. "A good girl like that? A future?"

Brian doesn't say anything, just slumps toward the passenger door.

"Well, I guess we know what part of you got left in Afghanistan," Dad snorts. "The part that used to be between your ears."

Though Dad talks to me like this all the time, I've never heard him speak to Brian this way before. I play possum until I'm sure the conversation is over for good, then yawn and stretch dramatically. From the view out the window when I sit up, I can see we've reached the outskirts of Longview.

I'm glad when both my dad and Brian are silent for the rest of the drive home.

THIRTY

*(ABC News)—Sixteen U.S. soldiers were killed
in Kunar Province after their helicopter was shot
down by insurgents. This represents the worst
one-day U.S. casualty record in the history of
Operation Enduring Freedom–Afghanistan.*

....

After the hunting trip, things start to go downhill at full
tilt. To everyone's surprise, Dad announces that he's taken
on a load that will require him to be away for two weeks.
"Maybe longer," he tells us gruffly. "Hard to say."

Mom doesn't argue, but her mouth tightens into a narrow line I've seen before.

I try, a couple times, to bring up to Dad what happened
on the trip, but he doesn't seem to want to talk about it.
"Dov, your brother just lived through a helluva bad experience. He just needs some time to settle things in his mind.
And don't you go making him feel like he's some kind of
nutcase," Dad warns, giving me a hard look.

I go away wondering how everything is always turned around on me.

These days, Brian's moods are swinging all over the place; sometimes he's the familiar, upbeat Brian, and other times he's downright nasty. He no longer makes any effort to hide his drinking; if Mom notices the bottles stacking up in the trash can before I haul it out back, she doesn't say anything. She seems more worried by the fact that Brian and Victoria seem to be arguing all the time.

"I don't even know what to say to him anymore, Dov," Victoria told me tearfully one night. I got caught in the kitchen when she came stumbling up from the basement, crying. "Nothing I do is ever right. He's just not the same person he was before he left."

I wish I knew what to tell her, but I don't. At night, I often hear Brian prowling through the house. Sometimes I hear the back door being softly unlatched, then opened and closed. I can only guess that my brother is out patrolling the neighborhood, alert for signs of insurgents, stepping carefully to avoid IEDs. It makes me sick with fear to imagine what might happen if he encounters anyone he thinks is suspicious, especially since I figure it's a sure thing he's carrying the pistol I saw in his duffel.

Even when he seems calm, I know that inside, Brian is tense and wary, like a cat poised to spring. Just looking at him, I can see that his mind is always busy, and yet he accomplishes almost nothing. When he blows off his admissions testing appointment at the university, even Mom is driven to snap at him in frustration. For the most part, though, we're all tiptoeing around him, sensing he's a short, fraying fuse that no one wants to light.

Besides worrying constantly about Brian, the rest of my attention is on Leo, who's continuing his slow belly-crawl toward starvation. It's become clear that things with him are serious. Finally, I break down and go to the local pet store, where I talk to Jared, the kid in charge of reptiles. "You could try and tempt his appetite," Jared suggests.

"How do I do that?" In the past, Leo's diet was pretty simple: crickets, crickets, and more crickets.

Jared leads me to a large bin in the back of the store, near the sinks. "These are a little pricier than crickets," he says, reaching his hand down into the bin, "but they usually do the trick." He shows me his palm, on which writhe a pile of plump, blind-looking creatures. "Mealworms," he says. "They're loaded with fat and cholesterol so we don't recommend them as part of a regular diet, but they usually work in emergencies."

I considered the squirming mass of bacon-double-wormburgers. "You think these will work, huh?"

"Don't they look irresistible?"

They actually look pretty resistible to me, but I shrug and listen as Jared tells me how to keep the mealworms fresh. "Feed 'em some oatmeal and wheat germ," he says. "Put them in a shoebox with some egg cartons and they'll be in heaven."

"And if this *doesn't* work?"

Jared sighs. "Sometimes geckos just stop eating and need to be reminded to start again before they get too weak. Once that happens, they don't have the energy to hunt down their food anymore. Your last resort would be to force-feed him, and you won't want to wait too much longer."

I hope it wouldn't come to that. I don't relish the idea of prying open Leo's beaky mouth to force a writhing meal worm down his throat.

Jared's expression is grim. "The worst-case scenario is that he's impacted. Sometimes the system gets, uh ... corked. Then not much you *can* do."

There's no need to ask him to elaborate. I head home to begin Operation Mealworm.

At least at school, there's something else to think about besides the trouble at home; all our minds are on the upcoming concert. It's hard to believe that in only a few days, we'll be in the same room—okay, it's a coliseum—as Poisoned Heart.

"We should leave by five," Ali proposes at lunch, the week before.

"Yeah," says Miranda. "We want to make sure we can get close to the stage." There's no such thing as "seating" at concerts like this; everyone stands.

"What's the official emo tree?" the noxious voice of Ray Sellers calls from a few tables away. None of us even glance his direction, but that doesn't deter him.

"Weeping willow!" Ray shouts. The idiots at his table erupt in laughter, and I can't help but notice that a few others in the lunchroom chuckle as well.

"Let's all meet at Dov's at four-thirty," Koby proposes.

"The concert doesn't start until nine, so that should give us plenty of time."

"I've got some bad news," I announce glumly. "I can't drive."

Brian has already commandeered the Gator for this weekend, leaving me without wheels. Some of his buddies from boot camp are coming through town, and he wants to show them a good time. I know better than to suggest to anyone at my house that the concert is more important.

Everyone looks crestfallen. "I can try to get my mom's car," Koby says finally. "I'll convince my shrink it's important to my mental health for me to go. He'll talk to her."

I wonder how much of Koby's crap his shrink *really* buys into, but I'm relieved that we have a possible alternative mode of transportation.

"What about you, Scarlett?" Miranda asks. "Should we pick you up?"

"Uh, sure." Scarlett nods. Even though she's smiling, I know she's nervous about going out of town with us all. "You guys have been friends for so long," she told me during one of our phone calls. "It's hard to really feel like I fit in."

I told her not to worry about that, but the truth is, I know what she means.

Scarlett is definitely trying harder with all of us lately, but it's clear that she still feels like the outsider in our group, even with me. Maybe we can all feel how she's holding back, so it makes us do the same. It's kind of a trust thing, I guess.

I've opened up some to Scarlett about the things that

are going on with Brian. Besides Ali, she's the only one who knows. Somehow, the fact that she didn't know the old Brian Howard makes it seem like less of a betrayal. She thinks that Brian's problems might be something called post-traumatic stress disorder. "Seriously, I've heard of it," she told me. "Lots of soldiers have problems with it when they come back from war. You should talk to Mr. Kerr— maybe he can give you some advice."

I don't want to imagine Mom and Dad's reaction if they find out I've told the school counselor that my brother, the pride of Longview High, has fallen into the deep end of the crazy pool. All I can do is just hope Brian won't drown.

Now everyone at the lunch table is discussing how much gas will cost for the trip from Longview to Milford and back, and how much money we should bring for T-shirts, CDs, water, etc. "And for food," Miranda reminds us. "For after." It's a given that we'll leave the Poisoned Heart concert feeling giddy, a little deaf, possibly banged up from moshing, and starving... it'll only make sense to rehash the best night of our lives over plates of greasy food in some roadside diner on the way home.

"Man, it's going to be so sweet," Koby predicts for the millionth time.

When I get home after school, Brian's conked out on the couch. His late-night wanderings leave him exhausted during the day, and he's taken to napping on the couch in the late afternoons. Actually, "napping" is a weak description of what my brother does with his eyes closed. "*They're coming in checkpoint... 323 have copy?*" he's muttering now. "*Can anyone confirm reports of SA-6 south of Mir Bacha Kot? Go ahead, go ahead, we got you up here…*"

From the top of the recliner where she's sunning herself, Sheba raises an eyebrow at me. "I know, right?" I tell her, shaking my head.

I'm finishing an after-school bowl of cereal at the kitchen table when Brian appears in the doorway. "Hey," he says, running a hand through his hair. He looks terrible: dark, smudged crescents have appeared under his eyes, and his skin, which was tanned and ruddy when he arrived home, now looks sallow and unhealthy. Shaving has become a random act, and the stubble on his face makes him seem unwashed, a long way from the thin-but-clean-shaven soldier who came walking toward us in the Longview airport. He's even stopped wearing his eye patch most of the time and his discolored and bloodshot eye is so disturbing that I heard Mom timidly ask him to put it back on.

Now he slides into one of the kitchen chairs and leans back, stretching his arms over his head. It's good to see him have full use of them again. "What's happenin'?"

"Not much. You?"

Brian yawns. "Well," he says, "looks like I'm single and ready to mingle."

"Seriously?" He's managed to shock me. "Victoria broke up with you?" If Brian was on the edge before, I can't imagine what this is going to do to him.

My brother shrugs. "Naw, I broke it off," he says, as casually as if he was telling me he just changed the oil in the Gator, not kicked the hottest girl in the world to the curb.

"But ... *why?*" They were the perfect couple—the Jack and Diane of Longview. When they got engaged, the Longview Herald ran a feature about them in the "Notable Engagements" section. "What about the wedding?" I ask stupidly.

"Obviously there's not going to be one, dumbass."

"Mom's going to kill you."

Brian frowns. "Yeah. I know."

We're both silent for a minute. "I mean ... what's going on, Brian?" I say finally.

He puts his elbows on the table and steeples his fingers together like he's about to say something important. I wait expectantly, really wanting him to explain everything, to make it all make sense. To tell me there's been a mix-up and that Brian Howard, Human Being Extraordinaire, will be arriving in Longview on the next plane.

"It just wasn't right," he says finally, shrugging again.

"What? You and Victoria?"

"I don't know." Brian grimaces. "Me and Victoria ... me and this place ... me and *life*. Face it, Dov; I just don't fit with anything anymore."

"Yes, you do," I tell him. "It's just going to take time—"

"NO!" Brian explodes. "It's not that easy! When I was over there, I was part of something ... meaningful. I mean, no offense, bro, but this stuff that goes on here ... it's a fucking *joke*."

Suddenly I'm furious. Everyone has bent over backwards to try and make Brian's return as easy on him as possible. Heck, I even went *hunting*. And not only does my new, *asshole* brother not appreciate any of it, but he isn't even trying to make things work.

"Really," I shoot back at him. "So we're all a fucking joke to you, huh?"

Brian doesn't respond to my question; he barely seems to see me at all as he pushes back his chair and gets up to pace around the kitchen. "That's not what I said. And I know everyone's trying, but no one can see that I'm a completely different person than the Brian Howard who left here nine months ago. Dude, that guy was an *idiot*!" my brother rants. "A pathetic tool who thought he had it all figured out … football, college, Victoria … such a simple plan. But now everything's different." He turns and focuses intently on my face, like he's going to tell me something that he wants to make sure I hear. "I seem like I'm here, but I'm not, Dov. I'm in a totally different space. It's like … no man's land."

"No man's land," I repeat. "What's that supposed to mean?"

"You wouldn't understand."

"So explain it to me then," I demand. "If we're all just too goddamn lame to 'get you,' then why don't you tell me what we're missing?"

Brian leans against the kitchen counter. His eyes travel away from my face and over my shaggy hair, my Paramore T-shirt, my dark Bullhead jeans and black tennis shoes. "I know *you* get it," he says softly, nodding toward me.

"What are you talking about?"

"You know … the stuff you wear, your hair, your whole 'darkness' thing."

I shake my head, confused.

"That's me," Brian says simply. "That's what I am. You're just strong enough to show it on the *out*side."

A moment of silence stretches between us. "Brian," I say, leaning forward to make sure he's listening to me now. "Don't you think maybe you're depressed or something? Maybe you should see a doctor."

"Depression is just a word, man, a small, meaningless word."

"But if you tell Mom … "

"Yeah, right," he chuckles. "Mom and Dad don't want to hear about this. All they want is for me to be the old Brian, the football-star-gonna-marry-the-mayor's-daughter-and-someday-maybe-own-his-own-business Brian Howard. Am I right?"

I'm silent. To my surprise, a moment later Brian leans down and throws an arm around me. The way he smells tells me he hasn't showered today, or maybe yesterday either. "I love you, bro," he says, his breath sour, his cheek rough and scratchy against mine.

Straightening up, he adds, "Whatever the hell that means."

I sit there helplessly and let him walk away.

THIRTY-ONE

(CNN)—Thirteen Americans were killed in two helicopter crashes yesterday, bringing the number killed this month to 55. Officials said that the attacks involved "multiple, complex bombs," raising the fear that Al Qaeda's weaponry is becoming more sophisticated and lethal…

....

It's Saturday afternoon, over a week since Jared the Lizard Guy gave me his input. If Leo has eaten anything at all since then, it sure doesn't show in the gauntness around his midsection. Even so, I'm still trying to put off the idea of force-feeding him.

"Tomorrow morning," I threaten. "If you haven't started eating on your own by then, you and I have a breakfast date, and I have the feeling neither one of us is going to enjoy it."

Leo regards me balefully.

"I'm serious," I tell him.

We should talk, Grasshopper… Leo begins tiredly.

"Dov!" Mom calls. "Your friends are here."

"Okay!" I yell back, feeling a rush that the long-awaited day has finally arrived. In a few short minutes I'll be in the Buick with everyone else, heading toward our rendezvous with Poisoned Heart.

"Look," I say to Leo sternly. "I'm done talking. Tomorrow, amigo, we're eating."

Before I leave, I check myself out one last time in the mirror. After much deliberation, I decided to wear my skinniest Bullheads, a studded belt, black Converses, and a new black T-shirt from the Dusty Groove. My hair is growing out nicely, and I added a smudge of guy-liner for the occasion.

"What time will you be back?" Mom asks as I come through the kitchen.

"Honestly, Mom, I have no idea," I tell her. "Can we not do the curfew thing tonight?"

Mom considers. "I suppose," she says finally. "Just promise me … well, just be careful."

"I will." I watch her take everything in and decide to bite her tongue, which I appreciate.

Brian is already gone; his boot camp buddies arrived mid-afternoon, their loud voices audible from the basement as they compared notes on where they'd been and what they'd seen. When they left in the Gator, Brian was in a better mood than I've seen him in since he came back to Longview.

From outside, the Buick's horn lets me know my friends are impatient to get going.

"Later," I tell Mom, who waves me off with a sigh.

"If you didn't show up in about ten seconds we were gonna leave without you," Miranda informs me over her shoulder when I pull open the Buick's heavy door and climb into the back seat. She's riding shotgun while Ali, Scarlett, and I are in the back seat.

"You'd never leave me," I say. "I'm the brains of this operation." That prompts a barrage of friendly abuse, and I settle back against the seat, grinning.

"Hey," says Scarlett. She looks especially pretty tonight with her hair held back by two small flowered clips. Ali has gone out on a fashion limb, with red eye shadow and a checkered flannel shirt. I imagine his parents watching him leave the house, their dark heads inclined toward one another in pride and fascination.

Koby backs down the driveway and onto the street. From the front, Miranda turns and holds up her cell phone. "Everyone get closer together," she orders; we do, and she snaps a pic to document the occasion.

"Send it to me," I ask.

"Me too," Scarlett echoes.

We drive across town toward the highway that leads to Milford; passing Marhoola's bar, I'm surprised to see the Gator parked in the lot.

"Hey Dov, isn't that your car?" Miranda asks.

"Yeah," I admit. "My brother has it tonight. Some of his Guard buddies are in town."

Koby pulls to a stop at the light. "I heard Brian broke

it off with Victoria Hart," he says, looking at me in the rearview. Clearly news of the broken engagement is making its way across Longview. "Is he nuts?"

I shrug. "He's sort of … not himself these days. I don't think he knows what he's doing."

"I'll say," Koby agrees. "That chick's hotter than Megan Fox."

There's a general murmur of agreement. I don't join in, hoping the subject will die.

"Turn up the radio," I instruct Miranda as we pull onto the highway. This is going to be a great night, one we've all looked forward to for a long time, and there's no way I'm going to let anything, much less Brian, ruin it.

The Milford Coliseum is already buzzing with activity by the time we turn into the east access of the parking lot. Dark-haired kids in tight clothes and colorfully dressed kids with wide belts and bright hair swarm everywhere; it's like an emo/screamo extravaganza. Loud speakers play songs from Poisoned Heart's latest album, getting everyone in the mood, as if we hadn't all been *born* in the mood for this concert.

Finding a parking spot is a challenge, but Koby finally spots one on the outer fringes. Even from this distance, we can hear the music in the still night air. "I can't wait to get in there!" Miranda squeaks, doing a little skip beside me.

"Me neither," I agree. "It's going to be awesome."

Miranda has gone really intense with her red hair tonight; it's ratted a mile high, like a character from *The Rocky Horror*

Picture Show. To top it off, she's wearing black cotton fishnet stockings and striped legwarmers; I wonder how girls think of these things. "You look really pretty," I tell her, leaning over to say it directly into her ear.

Surprise blooms on Miranda's face. "Thanks," she says, smiling. "You look good too."

Outside the Coliseum, we stop for a minute to catch our breath. "Check it out," Ali says, nodding toward a throng of scene kids in bright T-shirts. They're hardcore dancing, their arms flailing and spinning.

"Someone's going to dislocate a shoulder," Scarlett comments dryly.

Ali nods. "Looks like they're having a group seizure."

Miranda leans toward me. "Why are scene kids so bad at karate?" she asks.

"Why?"

"Because they can never get beyond the white belt."

"Ha." I laugh, feeling great, happier than I've felt in a long time.

"Hey, Dov," Miranda says, her voice so quiet I have to lean close to hear. "I've kind of been meaning to ... "

Suddenly Scarlett appears beside us, interrupting. "Should we go inside?" she asks. I check my phone and see that it's nearly seven; from inside come the sounds of the opening band, Moby Dick, playing their first notes right on cue.

"Yeah," I agree, "let's go in. Definitely." As we follow Scarlett, Ali, and Koby into the current of bodies flowing through the coliseum's massive doors, I grab Miranda's hand, not letting us get separated.

Inside, we lose ourselves in a throng of kids with long bangs and sprayed, ratted, or dyed hair. Moby Dick's first number, "Eskimo," is phenomenal; their stuff makes me think of Samiam and Still Life. The mosh pit swings into action, pulsing and throbbing as kids flail and shove and run at each other. Periodically, small clearings are made for the dancers who compete to impress each other and the crowd. Making room for them is the only way to avoid getting seriously hurt by their violent windmills and spin kicks. For reasons unknown to anyone, part of hardcore dancing is trying to appear as if you have absolutely no concern for the well-being or safety of anyone around you. This sometimes leads to injury ... I've once seen a guy take a serious elbow to the forehead when he got too close to a kid who was "picking up change"—standing with his feet shoulder-width apart and brutally punching at the ground.

Every so often, a mosher is involuntarily ejected from the fray, only to be caught by random onlookers and boomeranged back in. Along the pit's fringes, scene kids are whirling around safely, smiling at each other and doing their happy little dances.

The non-moshing contingent stays out of harm's way for the most part, content to bob their heads to the music and snap pictures with their phones. Later tonight, there will be thousands of uploads to hundreds of LiveJournals and Facebook pages.

Miranda pulls at my arm. When I lean down, she yells "*Sah-weet*," into my ear, or at least I think that's what she says. The music is so loud it feels like it's coming from inside my head, and the place is getting warm from the crowd's body heat. I look around for Scarlett and see her standing a few feet away with Ali and Koby; her eyes are closed and she's pumping her fist to the beat of the music.

Satisfied, I turn my attention back to the band. None of the five band members are much older than we are, yet they're opening for Poisoned Heart. *It must be amazing to have your life come together like that,* I think.

Two songs later they finish their set to enthusiastic applause and leave the stage. Roadies come out to pack up their gear and the crowd begins milling around, shaking off sweat and talking in loud voices in order to cut through the ringing in everyone's ears.

"I need air," Scarlett says, her voice tinny and far away. "Want to come with me?"

"Sure."

I break a path through the crowd as we thread our way toward the concessions. People seem to be moving in currents; I feel Scarlett curl a finger through one of my belt loops so as not to get separated from me.

The line at the concessions stand is long, and the one at the T-shirt stall is even longer. "Let's go outside," I tell her. "We can come back later."

She nods. "It's *so* frickin' hot in here."

Outside gives us immediate relief; the cold, clean air

feels amazing in my lungs. I breathe in deeply, cooling myself from the inside out.

Scarlett is gazing up at the sky, her eyes soft. "I love nights like this," she says, walking a few steps away. "When the sky is so clear that you can see every single star. Most nights you never realize how many are up there."

I look up to see it the way she did. "Yeah," I say. "I guess I've never thought about that before."

"It makes me think of summers when I was, like, eight. My mom would pack food and we'd drive out to the lake and spend the whole day out there. I'd run all over the beach looking for interesting pieces of driftwood, fossils, whatever. At the end of the day, Dad would build a fire and we'd make hot dogs and s'mores and watch the sunset. And then the stars would come out."

The blackness of the sky expecting stars... the line from *Polychrome* pops into my head. I still haven't asked Scarlett about the poems. She hasn't mentioned them, and for some reason that makes me unable to bring them up. Until now. "Hey, Scarlett," I say, "I've been meaning to ask you—"

"There you are!" Koby's coming toward us, his sweaty blond hair sticking to his forehead. "No one knew where you guys went. The band's going to start any minute."

"We came out here to cool off a little," I tell him. I'm kind of bummed that the moment has passed to ask about the poetry bombs.

Koby nods appreciatively. "It does feel awesome out

here," he agrees, shaking his head violently enough to send the sweat flying. Scarlett backs out of range, but she's smiling.

"Are you glad you came?" I ask her.

"A hundred percent," she says. "I'm so glad Miranda invited me along."

"Miranda's awesome," Koby agrees. Even though he's addressing Scarlett, for some reason he's looking at me.

"Yep," I second.

We stand there quietly for a minute or two, studying the sky and enjoying the night air. A smattering of snowflakes drift down from the sky and we have a contest to see who can catch more of them on their tongue.

"Man, I need more than this to drink," Koby says finally. "Too bad the line to buy water is like a mile long."

"I don't mind," Scarlett says. "I'll go get us all some."

"Better hurry," I advise. "It can't be long before Poisoned Hearts comes out."

Koby and I dig in our pockets for money and Scarlett sets off.

"She's pretty decent too," Koby comments as we watch her walk away. "Not like she seemed at first."

"Yeah." I know my friends have given Scarlett another chance because of me, because they care about and trust me. It's so different from how I feel at home.

All of a sudden, the unmistakable strains of Poisoned Heart's opening number issue forth from inside the Coliseum.

"Damn!" Koby exclaims. "I wanted to see them come out!"

"No big deal." I shrug. "We can catch Scarlett on the way."

We head inside to get what we came for.

THIRTY-TWO

....

Poisoned Heart doesn't disappoint; the music is tight and the band makes sure to cover both of their albums, playing a sweet mix of old and new stuff. The mosh pit swings back into action; bottles of water and other, sweeter beverages start arcing through the air. It isn't long before the floor is both wet and sticky, but miraculously, no one falls. Crowd surfers spring up and a Wall of Death forms briefly, but Security steps in and it quickly flames out.

Even with all the action on the floor, Poisoned Heart's sound is amazing—every breakdown pumps new energy through the crowd.

"I hope they play 'Sanctuary'!" Miranda shouts.

I try to reply, but between the pulse of the music and the pounding in my head, it's impossible to tell if any sound is coming out of my mouth or not. I've downed the bottle of water Scarlett managed to buy, but the place is like a sauna and I'm sure I've probably sweated it all out already. Just as I decide I have to head back outside or I'll pass out, the band cues up the opening bars of "Sanctuary."

> *I will build myself a castle*
> *Hang a bright sun in the sky*
> *Fill the fields with golden flowers*
> *Pour a crystal lake nearby*
> *I'll construct a stony fortress*
> *Where I cannot hear your lies*
> *And then hide myself inside it*
> *So you'll never see me cry*
> *Sanctuary . . . sanctuary . . .*

It's surreal hearing the words coming straight from the band that wrote them. Miranda grabs my arm; when I look at her, she has tears of happiness in her eyes. "I can't believe we're actually here," she hollers in my direction, or at least that's what I think she says.

Rather than attempt any words, I grab her hands in mine and we grin at each other with pure joy. It's doubtful that any other night of my life will be able to top this one.

> *I'll lock my heart away from you*
> *That precious piece of glass*
> *Send a messenger with my farewell*
> *This pain will be my last*
> *Sanctuary . . . sanctuary . . .*

Too soon, it's over. The band plays two encores, but it still isn't long before we're being swept along in the wave of dazed, happy, and nearly deaf people flowing out of the Coliseum. We chatter all the way back to the car, laughing at how odd and distant our own voices sound to our damaged ears.

Finally, we reach the Buick and stand around smiling tiredly at each other while Koby finds his keys. With the doors unlocked, everybody collapses inside. Despite the great time we've had, it's a relief not to be jostled and buffeted by total strangers.

"Whoa," Ali says, after we've been quiet for a few seconds.

"Yeah," I agree, thinking Ali has pretty much nailed it, and Scarlett nods in agreement.

"Totally awesome," Koby sums up.

Miranda sighs happily. "Anyone else starving?"

It isn't until much later, after we've filled our bellies with truck-stop food and piled back into the car for the long ride home, that I look at my phone: *Four missed calls.*

Quickly, I fumble with the buttons, reviewing the history. I've missed four calls all right. And every one of them is from Victoria.

THIRTY-THREE

*(**ABC News**)—A radio-controlled model truck sent to one soldier by his younger brother likely saved the life of Staff Sgt. Christopher Fessenden. Fessenden and his platoon used the toy to check the road ahead of them on a patrol, and were surprised when it became tangled in a trip wire connected to an estimated 500 pounds of explosives. The bomb went off, sparing the lives of six soldiers controlling the truck from their Humvee...*

....

I'll never know whether it happened while we were watching Poisoned Heart or while I was chowing down on pancakes and eggs at the I-94 Café and Truck Stop, but sometime during the night, Brian got pulled over by an alert police officer. Victoria told me that the cop gave him a breathalyzer test and arrested him for driving under the influence of a controlled substance. It doesn't matter what the controlled substance was, although since I'd seen the

Gator at Marhoola's, I figure Brian and his friends had met up with Brian's new best buddy, Jack Daniels.

When I get home, I find Brian sitting upright on the sofa in the darkened living room, looking ready to face a firing squad. On the positive side, he seems to be mostly sober.

"Hey," I say. "I talked to Victoria."

"Yeah," he says. "Her dad bailed me out."

I can only imagine how humiliated Brian must be to have been bailed out by his ex-future-father-in-law. "Is Mom up?" I ask.

"No," he says. "She doesn't even know yet. I figure I'll let her sleep. She'll need her energy to be ashamed of me in the morning."

There's really nothing I can say to that.

"God," Brian moans, burying his face in his hands. "How could I be so fucking stupid?"

I open my mouth, but can't really come up with anything that makes sense. "I don't know," I tell him finally. "It happens, I guess."

"Not to me," Brian sighs. "This isn't something that's supposed to happen to me."

He looks so lost and hopeless it worries me. "Look," I say, "right now there's no point thinking about it. I'm completely shot and I'm sure you are too. Let's just go to bed; we'll figure it all out in the morning."

"Yeah," Brian says, his voice flat. "Mom'll have to give you a ride to the cop shop and get the Gator. They towed it there."

"Okay. We'll get it figured out. Let's just go to bed."

Brian nods, but continues to sit there until I get up and reach out to pull him off the couch. His hand in mine is as cold as death, and he wobbles slightly before he gets his footing and I feel okay letting him go.

I go to my room and pull off my clothes, too tired to even to think about brushing my teeth. I'm half asleep before my head even hits the pillow, but one last image drifts through my mind and brings me hurtling back to wakefulness: Brian, downstairs in his bedroom, alone, humiliated, and depressed. The pistol is in his hand.

I bolt out of bed and run, through the kitchen and down the stairs. "Bri?" I call softly, not wanting to startle him under whatever circumstances I might be walking into.

The Howard basement has always been a comfortably disorganized place, but Brian's room is neat as a pin these days. His duffel has been unpacked, folded up, and tucked under his bed. His dress uniform hangs neatly in his closet, behind which the rest of his shirts are filed with regimented precision. To my relief, a quick glance at the bed reveals my brother, lying on his back and breathing heavily. He's in the deep, drugged-like sleep of the exhausted and inebriated.

I creep around in the dark, searching until I find the pistol tucked just underneath the bed, within easy reach. Even though I know there's a chance Brian might wake up in the night to look for it, I'm not about to take any chances. Holding the pistol securely in two hands, I carry it out of his bedroom and upstairs, where I bury it in the bathroom closet behind a stack of towels.

Back in my room, I make a decision: tomorrow I'm

going to talk to Mom and tell her everything I know about what's going on with Brian. Faced with all the evidence, it's hard to imagine she won't listen to what I have to say. And with my mind made up, I fall into my own deep, dreamless sleep.

————————

The next morning my mind revs into gear before I even wake up. Making the decision to talk to Mom brought me immense relief last night, but now that it's morning, I'm nervous. The truth is, in the past, my parents never really put much stock in what I had to say; I seldom gave them any reason to. Now I don't know whether Mom will take me seriously.

Nevertheless, I have to try. Sitting upright makes me feel tired all over again, so I lie back down to finish waking up. As I do, my eyes focus on the aquarium across the room and I remember what else Leo and I had planned for this morning.

"Guess what?" I call to Leo. "Today's the day that your hunger strike officially comes to an end."

I figure he'll have a few sarcastic retorts to that, but there's nothing. "Look, don't give me the silent treatment," I say. "You and I both know we've got to do something. Things can't go on like this." I sit up and swing my feet out of bed, then walk over so I can look at him while I talk about this. "I'll do the best I can to ... "

Leo's warming rock is bare, and he isn't lying in his water dish or anywhere out in the open. I nudge aside a pile of bark where he sometimes likes to hide, discharging a torrent of scurrying crickets, but no Leo. A few shriveled mealworms are scattered around on the substrate, which tells me he hasn't been eating them.

"Buddy?" I call softly. "Don't be like that. Come on, let's..." I lift up Leo's cave, and there he is.

His eyes are open but unmoving, their surfaces milky and dull. "Dude?" A feeling of unreality washes over me; from somewhere distant, I hear my heart begin to pound. Frantically, I toss the cave aside and use my finger to give Leo a sharp poke; he shifts a little, but stiffly, like a cardboard cutout version of Leo.

"No!" I gasp, too horrified to believe what my eyes are telling me. Gingerly, I pick up his body, but it's as lifeless and brittle as a twig on the sidewalk. Turning him over, I see that Leo has grown so emaciated that his stomach is practically glued to his backbone. Worst of all, it looks like the crickets turned the tables and nibbled most of the skin off of my friend's familiar crooked tail.

I carefully set Leo down on the desk next to the aquarium, trying hard to breathe. Seeing him loose outside his enclosure is strange, but there's no danger of him running away now. "I was going to ... feed you this morning," I tell him, the words barely squeezing their way past the painful lump in my throat. Tears prickle in my eyes and I wipe at them angrily with my palms. I'm not sure who I'm mad at: Leo or myself. "Why?" I demand. "Why couldn't you have hung on a little longer?"

Suddenly everything washes over me in a huge wave,

and my knees go weak under the pressure of it all. I stumble backwards and land on the edge of my bed, lurching with silent sobs. Through the hard times of the past, Leo was always there with his wry comments. Now, when things are at their worst, he's gone.

I think I cry for twenty minutes or more; every time it feels like the pain is subsiding, I lift my head and see what's left of Leo, or think of Brian's lost, defeated face in the darkness last night, and a new wave of tears comes from somewhere.

Suddenly, a warm hand is on my shoulder. "Dov … honey … what in the *world* is the matter?"

It's Mom, standing over me, her face pained with worry. Even though I've seen her face look worried before, this time it's for me, and the sight of it brings a fresh onslaught of tears. When she sees that I'm incapable of talking, Mom sits down on the bed beside me. She puts her arms around me and presses my head into her shoulder. "It's okay, sweetheart," she says. "Cry it out and then we'll talk."

Obediently, I cry until my breath comes in hiccups, and although it seems impossible, Mom is right: eventually I run out of tears.

OBITUARY

It is with great sadness that Dov Howard announces the passing of his beloved friend, Leo the Gecko. Leo arrived in the Howard household as a special gift on June 23, 2007 and passed away quietly, on his own terms, on December 4, 2011. During his lifetime, Leo provided all who met him with dry wit and quiet friendship, and served as a reminder of the joy of simple things: fresh crickets, a warm, sunny rock, and a relaxing swim in one's own pool.

From the very moment he arrived, Leo was the epitome of a faithful companion and sage advisor. His wisdom knew no boundaries, and he observed the world outside his enclosure with an objective and thoughtful eye.

Leo is survived by his wingman and human brother, Dov Howard. He will be missed beyond what Dov's mere words could ever express.

THIRTY-FOUR

*(American Psychologist)—Suicides among soldiers
continue to increase. The U.S. Army has reported
yearly increases for the past five years, with the toll
reaching 147 in the first eleven months of 2009.
Figures released by the Army reveal that about
one-third of these suicides involved soldiers who
were deployed at the time of their deaths, and
another third involved soldiers who had
returned from deployment…*

....

"I don't get it," Scarlett says, incredulous. "She didn't believe you?"

"It's not that she didn't believe me," I tell her, stabbing a straw into my cheeseburger. Scarlett is working at the Pepper now, so I came by hoping she'd be here. "It was just that the minute she heard about Brian breaking up with Victoria, tears started rolling down her face and she wasn't even listening after that." Frankly, I was surprised to see that Mom didn't already know about Brian and Victoria—

she must be the only one in town who hadn't heard the news. I haven't even told her about Brian's DUI; I figure it's my brother's responsibility to break that one to her.

"So, what now?" Scarlett asks, watching me.

"I don't really know." I shrug wearily. "I'm starting to think that my parents see what's going on, but they just can't deal with it. It's easier to pretend that Brian's just 'adjusting' to being home, because if they admit that it's anything more whacked than that, they'd have to do something. And I don't think they have the first clue what that would be."

"Sometimes it's just easier to look the other way," Scarlett says quietly. "Especially when the truth is too hard to face."

"I guess." We sit silently for a beat.

"I'm sick of this subject," I say finally. "Let's talk about something else."

"Sure," Scarlett says.

The only other subject I don't want to touch is Leo, who's lying in state in a Kleenex box on my desk, cushioned by a layer of folded paper towels. Although she's sympathetic to my loss, Mom isn't happy about a dead animal in the house and she's after me to dig a hole in the backyard to bury him. I haven't been able to do it yet; if I even let myself think about what happened to Leo, a sledgehammer-blow of guilt nearly sends me to my knees. I know I shouldn't have waited so long to try and fix things for him. And yet, like I see happening with Brian and my parents, it's easier to deny how serious a problem is if acknowledging it means doing something you dread.

I hesitate. I did have an ulterior motive for dropping

in to visit Scarlett. Another poem has turned up, this time tucked into my History book. It's the darkest one yet.

> *Clinging to the wall of my abyss*
> *Curled fingers ache*
> *The dampness chills my bones*
> *Looking for a place to plant my weight*
> *I fumble blind across hardscrabble stone*
> *My teeth gnash hard together in my mouth*
> *The taste of blood explodes upon my tongue*
> *I slip and plummet down and down and down*
> *One faulty step and everything's undone.*

"Hold on a second," she says, seeing a customer come in. "I'll be right back."

I watch her go, thinking that this time I'm not going to lose my nerve. I want to talk to Scarlett about an idea I've had for her to submit one of her poems to the school newspaper, the *Longview Leader*. I'm sick of putting up with the harassment and judgments of morons like Ray Sellers, and I want him and everyone to see Scarlett's amazing talent. I'm not sure she'll go for it, though; if she has to give her poetry to *me* anonymously, I figure it'll take some major convincing to get her to publish it for the rest of the school to read. Still, I hope that once she sees how much everyone loves her work, she'll be more open about it. Miranda and I express our feelings through our drawing, but Scarlett gets hers out with words.

Things are getting busier at the Pepper and it's a good ten minutes before she's free again. Until then, I watch her smile and talk to customers as she waits on them. It's nice to see her smile, and she's been smiling a lot more lately. She's dyed her hair blond on top and black underneath. Even though it's dramatic, it looks happier, somehow. According to what she's told me, her mom said her dad was doing better. Scarlett hopes she'll be invited back home by Christmas, or maybe Easter.

She comes back to my table carrying a glass of soda. "I can take my break now," she says, sliding into the seat across from me.

I watch her peel the end of the paper from her straw. "So ... I want to talk to you about something."

She aims her straw at me and blows the wrapper in my direction, grinning when it nails me in the shoulder. "Sure. What's up?"

"I want to talk about the, uh, poems."

She tilts her head. "Poems?"

I almost expected this. "Scarlett," I say patiently, in a c'mon-we-both-know-what-I-mean voice. "The poems you write?"

Now it's Scarlett who hesitates. "What about them?"

"They're really good, Scarlett." I take a deep breath. "I think a lot of people would like them. So, I was thinking maybe you should submit some of them to the *Leader*. I know it sounds lame, but ... "

Scarlett raises her eyebrows. "The *Longview Leader*? Dov, I don't think it's really the type of stuff I want people to see."

"But the ones I've read ... "

Scarlett looks confused. "The ones *you've* read?" she

repeats. "What are you talking about?" Her face darkens. "Did Kerr show you my poems?"

"Kerr? I mean *Polychrome,* and the other ones ... the ones you put in my jacket, and my locker, and my ... "

"Poly-*what*?" Scarlett seems genuinely puzzled. "Dov, Mr. Kerr is the only person who's ever seen any of my poetry. He keeps them in a file in his office. They're all about ... well, *you* know ... the stuff that happened before I came here. Not stuff I want the whole school to read."

Now I'm the one who's confused. "But if you didn't write those poems ... then who did?"

She shrugs. "How would I know? Why did you think it was me in the first place?"

"I don't know ... I guess I just assumed it was you. It kind of started around the time you got here, and ... it was just something that seemed like you, I guess. They really are good," I add thoughtfully.

"Nope," Scarlett says. "Not me." She tilts her head to one side, curious now. "So someone's been slipping you poetry? Geez, Dov, who do you think it is?"

"No idea," I admit honestly. "None at all."

THIRTY-FIVE

....

Brian's DUI means that I'm stuck driving him everywhere, especially since Victoria is no longer in the picture. This is becoming problematic for both of us.

As if Mom isn't already upset enough about the DUI, now Brian has decided to postpone college for a while. This morning, he wants me to take him to Scheels to talk to Scott about getting his old job back. "Come *on*, Dov, let's go," Brian shouts from the living room. "Don't make me come in there and get you."

I'm in my room with Leo; it's been a week since he died, and it's clear I can't keep his body forever. With duct tape, I carefully seal him into his Kleenex box for the final time. *Zen Arcade,* Leo's favorite, is on the turntable.

Look, if it was impaction, nothing would have helped, Jared assured me when I confessed to him that I'd lost Leo.

In fact, force-feeding him would only have made him more miserable before he died, which is what ultimately would have happened.

I try to take comfort in that. "I'm sorry," I tell Leo's spirit for the hundredth time. "I'm really gonna miss ya, buddy."

No reply; the silence is deafening. I wish there was some way I could know whether Leo has forgiven me.

When I'm satisfied Leo is entombed properly, I leave his sarcophagus on my desk and snap off the record player, then head out to the living room, ready for orders. As usual, Brian is in a surly mood; Brian 2.0 seems to have an overactive irritability chip, and it's wearing Mom and me thin. "*Finally*," he snaps when he sees me.

Mom is reading a magazine on the couch and doesn't look up. It was Mom who informed me I'd been drafted as my brother's new chauffeur, adding that Dad has decided to stay on the road indefinitely. She hasn't mentioned our conversation about Brian again, but I found a pharmacy bottle in the bathroom cabinet with her name on it. *For Depression*, the label read.

I grab my keys and coat and follow Brian out to the Gator. There's no doubt winter has arrived; going out without a jacket now means risking hypothermia. It snowed a little last night, and I feel the Gator's tires skid on the slippery street as we head downtown.

"Have you talked to Victoria lately?" I ask Brian, searching for something to make conversation.

Brian grimaces. "No," he says shortly. "Why would you ask me that?"

"All right." I shrug. "My bad." Talking to my brother these days is like juggling active grenades; you never know when one is going to go off.

We ride on in safe silence until I finally pull into the Scheels lot. "Come back in about an hour," Brian orders. He straightens his eye patch, which these days qualifies as dressing up, before getting out and slamming the Gator's heavy door behind him.

"Yes *sir*," I mutter sarcastically.

I drive aimlessly downtown, figuring I'll stop in the Dusty Groove and look through the LPs. Since Christmas is coming, I figure they might have gotten some new stuff in.

Inside the store, I'm surprised and happy to see Miranda flipping through the used LPs. "Anything good?" I ask, coming up behind her.

Miranda turns and her face lights up. "Hey!" she says. She holds up a Rites of Spring album entitled *End on End*. "Look what I found."

"Wow, *sweet*." Rites of Spring was an 80s hardcore punk band, but a lot of their lyrics really make you think. I'd love to have *End on End* as part of my collection.

Miranda nods. "Jelly?"

"Um ... little bit."

"I know." She grins happily. "So what's up? You just come downtown to hang?"

"Nah, I had to give my brother a ride."

"He's still not driving?"

I shake my head. "No ... his eye. You know." The whole DUI thing makes me embarrassed. Even though everyone's adoration of Brian irritates me, there's something in me that likes having a brother who's pedestal-worthy. I guess there's a part of me that doesn't *want* people to see that he's losing it.

Miranda nods, but something in her face tells me she knows. I wish I'd been honest. "A lot has changed since he got back, hasn't it?" she says softly.

I lift my eyes to meet hers. "Kind of, yeah. Actually, pretty much everything."

"I know. I've been watching you. You seem different, Dov. Quieter. Even your art has changed. And you don't talk about Twohey as much."

I'm surprised; it isn't something I figure anyone noticed. The truth is, I do feel different lately.

Miranda sets the Rites of Spring album down and reaches out, taking my hand. Her nails are painted a dark peacock blue, and in her small, warm hand, mine look oversized and rough from the cold outside air. When she turns it over, we both look curiously at my palm, where I've written *NO MAN'S LAND* in red pen.

I expect Miranda to ask what it means, but she doesn't. I could have told her; I looked it up. According to Dictionary.com, it means "an area between opposing armies, over which no control has been established" and "an indefinite or ambiguous area where guidelines and authority are not clear."

That sounds about right.

"You can talk to me about anything, you know that right?" Miranda says now. "I would never tell anyone. Not even Koby or Ali. I'm your friend, Dov. Always."

I nod, surprised to find tears springing to my eyes. It's

something that seems to happen a lot lately, and it's embarrassing. I know Miranda has probably seen, but I pull my hand away and turn to flip rapidly through the used LPs, making myself focus on the selection. To her credit, Miranda acts as if she hasn't noticed anything, and we spend the next half hour browsing companionably through the Dusty Groove's latest inventory, talking music and comparing finds. By the time I leave to pick up Brian, I'm feeling a little better. Miranda pretty much always makes me feel that way.

THIRTY-SIX

....

I drive into the Scheels parking lot and am unsurprised to see Brian standing outside waiting, his hands shoved into the pockets of his bulky army-issue jacket. The sky overhead has darkened, and it's starting to snow. Brian's hair is already dusted with crystallized flakes, making him look prematurely gray.

"So, how'd it go?" I ask when he gets in the car.

Brian shrugs. "All right, I guess. Scott's going to think about whether he can use me."

"I thought he was holding your job for you. That's what Victoria said."

"Yeah, well," Brian says darkly. "I guess not."

I pull out of the lot and turn onto Main Street. "Don't go home," Brian suggests. "Let's just drive. I'm not up for parental interrogation yet."

The only thing I have planned for the rest of the day is to bury Leo in the half-frozen soil of the backyard, so a random drive sounds like a good way to put that off awhile longer. "Where?"

"Anywhere." Brian mumbles. "It doesn't matter."

We head down Main for a few blocks, then I turn right onto a side street and we drive up that. At the corner I take a left, then another right, taking us farther away from downtown. The snowflakes are growing larger and clinging together in loose clumps, but any of them that land wetly against the warm windshield dissolve immediately.

"One time, our unit came across this dead Afghan guy ... dude, he was huge," Brian says out of the blue. "He must have stepped on an IED or something; it blew him nearly in half. Like totally gutted, bro."

"Huh." By now I'm used to Brian's random stories of death and destruction.

"Usually they take their dead away, but I think this guy was just too big; he was just lying there with his eyes open and his arms up over his head, like he'd just given up. Or maybe they'd tried to drag him off and dropped him. Anyway, dude, for some reason, it kind of got to me. I mean, I still can see his face so clearly ... and that red-and-white-checked rag on his head. 'The Fat Man,' we called him, whenever it came up. 'The Fat Man.'"

As often happens after Brian recounts one of his terrible stories, I say nothing, but when I glance sideways, I see that my brother's mind is once again someplace far away. It's hard to imagine that my brother's eyes, only one of which still works properly, have witnessed such hideous things up close and personal. I wonder whether the eye behind the patch is constantly replaying those scenes for lack of anything else to look at; maybe that's why he rarely wears it anymore.

We drive past the Army recruiting office. "I've been doing some thinking," Brian says, staring at the red, white, and blue flag on the door. "The doctors think my eye might come back better than they thought. As soon as it's healed, I'm going to re-up."

Re-up; the only thing I can think of as Brian continues talking is a cop show I saw on television where the drug supplier said he had to go back to his crib and "re-up" his drug supply. *Great,* I think, *what's Brian into now?* I'm about to ask him whether he hasn't learned anything from his DUI, when the rest of what he's saying starts to sink in.

"The thing is, when I was talking to Scott today, it suddenly hit me: I don't belong here, Dov. The place I need to be … the only place I feel like *myself* … is back there. It's sort of its own universe, like that Stephen King book, *The Dome*. I thought real life was back home, but it isn't. Real life is back there … *inside* the bubble."

"Back there," I repeat. "So you're saying you want to go back to Afghanistan."

Brian nods. "Bro, I wanted to come home so bad, but I had no idea what it would be like, you know? I can't even talk to anyone about it, because no one really gets it. There's no one I can tell about half the shit that goes through my head or they'd lock me up, Dov, seriously. I've got to go back; it's the only thing that makes sense."

This is the second time I've heard Brian talk about looking to get deployed again, and suddenly I'm furious. Doesn't he realize what it was like for Mom and Dad, for *all* of us, when he was in Afghanistan? When we had to worry every second that we'd get word he'd been hurt or killed…and now he wants all of us to go back to that again?

"Are you *nuts*?" I explode. "If you go back there, Brian, it'll kill Mom. And Dad. You have no clue how freaked out we *all* were when you were over there."

"I can't think about that right now," Brian says. "The only thing I can think about is how miserable I've been ever since I got back."

"Of course you can't," I snap. "When do you ever think about anybody besides yourself?"

Now I have Brian's attention. "What did you say?" he demands angrily.

"Ever since you got home, you've been a selfish tool," I shout at him. "Half the time you're walking around biting everyone's head off, and the rest of the time you actually think you *are* back there." I haul in a deep breath. "Come to think of it," I spit, "maybe you *should* go back." As the words leave me, a wave of anger and adrenaline swells through my body. In response, my foot presses down hard on the accelerator so that the Gator surges forward, as if the car and I are one being.

Brian is opening his mouth to freak on me when out of nowhere, everything explodes: BAMM! Neither one of us is wearing a seat belt, and we both fly forward. My teeth slam into the hard curve of the Gator's big steering wheel, and Brian catapults up and onto the dash; his head colliding hard with the windshield and leaving behind a radiating spider web of cracks. An instant later, he rebounds back into his seat.

"RRmmm," Brian groans. My chin grows warm and wet, and my mouth fills with saliva and the coppery taste of blood. After a moment of frozen shock, I move my tongue gingerly against front teeth, which move loosely in their sockets. When I lift a hand to my mouth, it comes away covered in bright red blood, telling me I've split my lip.

"Y'okay?" I murmur to Brian. He raises his head and looks at me. I can see he's dazed, and there's a laceration etched across the golf-ball-sized lump rising on his forehead. Still, at least he's conscious and doesn't seem to be bleeding anywhere.

I shift in my seat and stretch my neck, trying to see over the Gator's steaming, crumpled hood. I have no idea what we hit, but as the air clears, I see it's another car; we broadsided it on the passenger side and as far as I can see, nobody inside is moving.

"Oh crap," I mutter, praying I haven't killed anybody. I struggle with the Gator's heavy door and when I finally get it open, I half-fall out onto the street.

Steam is rising from the Gator's engine, making it difficult to get a good look into the other car, but even through my shock something seems vaguely familiar. I take a few steps closer and see with horror that the passenger, a kid about my age, is slumped motionless in his seat. To my great relief, the driver is moving; as I watch, he turns and starts trying to rouse the kid.

All of the sudden, I realize why the other car looks familiar to me. *Oh my God*, I think. *It's not possible. It can't be them.*

But it is. The crumpled car jammed crosswise against the nose of the Gator is the gold-colored Hyundai sedan that usually sits in the driveway of the Gabol household. I've ridden in it myself when Ali's mom drives us to movies or drops me off at home after a sleepover. Which means that the man driving the other car is likely none other than Ali's dad, Dr. Gabol.

And the injured passenger is my best friend, Ali.

Fumbling for my phone, I pull it out of my jacket pocket with hands that are shaking so violently I can barely manage to push the buttons for 911.

THIRTY-SEVEN

....

"Dr. Gabol!" I shout, yanking on the driver's side door. "It's me, Dov! God, I'm so sorry..." The car's frame was twisted in the impact; the door is jammed and I can't get it to budge.

Dr. Gabol turns away from Ali, looking confused. "Dov?" he says, his voice muffled behind the window, "What are you doing here?"

"We had an accident," I tell him, near tears. "I hit you with my car. Can you help me get the door open?" *Why couldn't I have been the one hurt instead of Ali?*

"Ali has been injured," Dr. Gabol says in his formal way. "He's unconscious. I'm not sure what happened." Blood is coming from somewhere under his hair and running down onto his face. Absently, Dr. Gabol reaches onto

244

the seat beside him and picks up a winter scarf, wrapping it around his head to keep the blood out of his eyes.

"I know," I tell him, trying to be patient. "We had a car accident. I already called 911, so help is coming. Push on the door, okay? Please!" For some reason, I'm frantic to make sure they aren't trapped inside the car.

Obediently, Dr. Gabol turns toward the door and takes hold of the handle. "Your face... you are bleeding, Dov," he observes. "You may be seriously injured."

"I'm fine," I assure him. "Push!" Finally, Dr. Gabol seems to register what I'm asking him to do, and he obediently puts his shoulder against the door. I pull mightily, and with a creak of protest, the door reluctantly inches open.

The cold, fresh air that sweeps in seems to make Dr. Gabol more alert. "What happened, Dov?" he asks again.

"A car accident," I tell him, feeling more horrible every time I have to confess it. "I hit you. And Ali's hurt."

Dr. Gabol looks back at Ali, who's still not moving. "I should go for help," he says, then looks at me as if he needs permission.

"I already called 911," I repeat slowly. "They're on their way. We should stay right here."

Ignoring me, Dr. Gabol slides out of the driver's seat and stands up next to the car. He looks okay, but is clearly not thinking straight. "You stay here with my son," he instructs me. "I'll find someone to help us."

Rather than argue with him, I slide into the driver's seat next to Ali, who to my great relief has finally begun to moan and stir. "Ali," I tell him, "it's me, Dov. We were in an accident, but you're going to be okay." I prayed to God this is true.

"Mmmmmh," Ali murmurs, his eyes still closed. Distantly, I hear sirens. I slide partway out of the driver's seat and look around for Ali's dad, wanting to make sure he hasn't wandered off. My neck is stiffening and it's hard to turn my head all the way, but finally, out of the corner of my eye, I see Dr. Gabol.

He hasn't made it any farther than the Gator, where he's standing now, staring at something I can't see. "Dr. Gabol!" I call, sticking my head out of the car. "Ali's waking up!"

"Hands in the air, Haji motherfucker!" Brian yells. He emerges from behind the Gator, the pistol I hid in the linen closet pointed at the head of his hostage, Dr. Gabol.

Holy. Shit. My mind seems to have suddenly gone into stop-start action and can only manage to form thoughts one word at a time.

"Dad?" Ali calls weakly from the car. "God, my head … what's going on?"

Outside, Dr. Gabol lifts his hands slowly, obediently into the air. He turns toward me, his dark, questioning eyes on mine.

I leave Ali behind and ease the rest of the way out of the car. The door is still jammed, so I have to squeeze my body through the opening.

"You got one there too, Wilkie?" Brian calls. "Keep him covered; I can handle Johnny Jihad here."

"Brian … " I begin, moving slowly to a standing position. "I'm not Wilkie...I'm Dov. Your brother. Listen, man, this isn't what you think."

My brother's sweaty, tense face disappears and reappears from behind Dr. Gabol. He's moving around and twitching with energy; his agitated and unpredictable state scares me more than anything. "*Hoowah*!" he barks suddenly. "We bagged us a couple Al Qaeda bitches!"

I start walking toward Brian and Dr. Gabol, keeping my hands where Brian can see them. "We're in Longview, Brian," I call loudly, trying to keep my voice from shaking. "You remember my friend, Ali, right? That man there is Ali's dad. He's a good man, a teacher at the university, remember? We're in Longview, Bri. This is *Longview*."

"Must be a sniper somewhere around here!" Brian yells. "Look at you, Wilkie, you've been hit!"

"We had a car accident," I tell Brian calmly. "I crashed the Gator. Man, Dad's gonna be pissed, right? I hit my face on the steering wheel. We're in *Longview*," I repeat, listening desperately for the sirens, which sound closer. If I can just keep things under control until help arrives...

"Dov?" Without my noticing, Ali has managed to climb out of the car and is standing behind me. As I turn, his eyes travel from my face, across the Gator to where my brother is holding Dr. Gabol at gunpoint. "Dad?" he asks, confused.

"Watch your back, Wilkie!" Brian screams, his agitation increasing. "He's right behind you!"

The sirens that have been drawing closer are upon us now as an ambulance turns the corner, followed by a police car. An instant later, both screech to a stop and the sirens die, although the emergency lights continue to flash. As the doors of the police car fly open and officers spill out, a horror movie scene plays out in my mind: police with guns drawn, aimed at Brian, telling him to let the hostage go, Brian screaming back deliriously...

"Take cover, Wilkie, I've got a clear shot!" Brian screams, pulling the gun away from Dr. Gabol's head so he can aim it toward Ali. Then things really *do* go into slow motion.

"BRRRIIIAAAANNNN!" I shriek, as I watch Brian's thumb move to pull back the hammer of the pistol. My feet scramble for purchase on the slippery ground as I take off toward my brother at a dead run. "Nooooooo...!"

Distantly, I hear a shout from the direction of the rescue vehicles.

I make a final desperate lunge and am in midair when our eyes meet; Brian's are wide and menacing, and I can't imagine what he sees in mine.

A shot rings out. I scream, but I know the story of my life has played out yet again.

As usual, I am too late.

THIRTY-EIGHT

....

"So you're telling me, son, that your brother has been dis-
playing symptoms of combat stress ever since he got home?"
I've been in the interview room with the detective for two
hours, and I'm ready to be done.

"Yeah," I reply impatiently. "Look, can you tell me
how's he doing? Does anyone know?"

The officer shrugs. "From what I heard, he's going to
be fine," he tells me. "It was just a superficial wound. Our
officers are well-trained; even in a hostage situation, the
primary objective is for everyone to make it out alive."

I nod and take another sip of my water. Even though I
heard Brian yelling incoherently in the ambulance, still deep
in his flashback, I'd seen the spray of blood as someone shot
the gun out of Brian's hand. Something in me keeps insist-
ing he's been hurt more seriously than I'm being told.

"Where is he?" I ask. "When can I see him?"

"Still at the hospital," the detective tells me. "Once he's been treated, they'll either bring him back to the station so he can be charged, or admit him to the psychiatric unit. It's up to the doctors at the hospital to decide which is more appropriate."

"Is my mother there with him?"

"I'm afraid I have no idea. Listen, just stick with me for a few more questions and I think we can wrap things up here."

I sigh, my foot jiggling frantically below the table. It's been doing that ever since I sat down; I hope it won't become some kind of permanent tic. "All right. Let's just get this over with so I can get out of here."

"Since he's been back, has there been any attempt to get your brother the help he needs? Any involvement with the VA? Any psychiatric evaluation?"

I shake my head. "No," I admit. "I—I think we were all just hoping he'd get it out of his system and then he'd be okay." The words sound lame, even to me.

"Uh-huh." The detective makes a few notes on his legal pad. "And he's been in some trouble with alcohol recently, according to our database."

"Yes. He had a DUI."

"Habitual drinker?"

"No," I insist. "Not before this. He was really…" I hesitate. "He's always been pretty great, actually. The kind of guy anybody would wish they had for a brother." A montage of images play in my mind: the crowd at Longview High cheering as Brian runs for a touchdown, Brian grinning with pride as he watches me discover Leo, Brian's blissful expression as he hugs Victoria … it all seems so long ago. How did Brian put it? *Another lifetime in an entirely different universe.* Before my brother got lost in No Man's Land.

"All right, son," the detective says, pushing back his chair and standing up. "If we have any more questions for you, we'll give you a call."

"I can go now?"

He nods. "You can go now."

The officer and I walk together out of the interview room and down the hall. "You know," he says, "a lot of our soldiers are coming back with problems these days. We just have to find a better way to make sure they get the help they need."

I nod. "So no one gets hurt," I add.

"So no one gets hurt."

As we reach the front door of the police station, the detective puts a hand on my shoulder, suddenly friendly. "You take care, son," he tells me. "Your brother's going to be okay. But he's going to need your help."

———

The officer was partially right: Brian's hand is swollen and bloody, but only superficially wounded. After it was bandaged in the ER, he was interviewed by the psychiatrist on call, who determined that Scarlett has been right all along: Brian is suffering from severe post-traumatic stress disorder.

They don't put him in Longview Hospital's psychiatric unit, though; instead, they take him by police escort to the VA hospital in Milford.

"They say he might be there for weeks," Mom tells me tearfully when I catch up with her at the hospital, but I hear an unmistakable measure of relief in her voice.

Ali is in a hospital room somewhere upstairs; he's been admitted with a severe concussion and will be monitored overnight. I want to ask about going up to see him, but Mom thinks maybe I should wait.

"I think I'll head up there," Koby says. I'd called him for a ride from the police station to the hospital, and told him the whole story on the way over. He, at least, doesn't seem to hate me. "I'll give ya a call later and tell you how he's doing."

"Thanks," I say gratefully. The truth is, I'm not sure I'm ready to face Ali and his parents yet.

"I just feel so awful," Mom says with a sigh as we walk out to the Suburban. "I knew he was having a hard time, but…" She trails off for a moment, then takes a deep breath. "I guess I was so relieved he made it back to us in one piece that I just couldn't let myself admit that he still needs help."

"You weren't the only one," I tell her. "We all just wanted Brian to get back to being…well, *Brian*. None of us wanted to believe that he wasn't still the best thing about our family."

Mom looks at me strangely. "Dov," she says, "do you really think of Brian that way? As the best thing about our family?"

"It's pretty obvious, don't you think? I mean, I haven't exactly given him much competition."

"Oh, Dov," Mom says. "You and your brother . . . you're two totally different people."

"I'll say."

Mom laughs in spite of herself. A moment later she surprises me by throwing her arms around my shoulders and squeezing me to her in a tight hug. I'm not a huggy sort of guy, but I can't say I hate it when she keeps her arm around me the rest of the way to the car.

THIRTY-NINE

....

Later that night, I'm in my room listening to tunes and working on my self-portrait for Twohey's class. I'm still doing the preliminary pencil sketch, but I'll redraw the whole thing in ink to give it more impact. The Dov Howard in my sketch is a thin-shouldered figure in a black T-shirt, hands buried deep in his pockets, body curved around the center of the painting as if the artist captured him immediately after he'd been punched in the stomach. Because of this posture, his face is hidden under long, dark hair.

I'm struggling with the shading when there's a knock on my door. "*Entrez vous*," I mutter, thinking it's Mom. Usually I don't like to be interrupted when I'm drawing, but tonight my room feels too empty without Leo watching me from his aquarium.

To my surprise, it's Miranda who stands in the doorway. "Hey," she says. "What's up?"

I gesture toward the sketchpad. "Self-portrait," I say.

Miranda comes over to have a look. "Wow, Dov," she says admiringly. "I love it."

"Really? Thanks."

"Yeah. You can't see your face though," she remarks. "You're stealing my shtick."

"Symbolism," I remind her.

"'A metaphor for your lack of hope?'"

"More like 'open to interpretation.'"

"Ah, so it's a projective test," Miranda teases. She sinks down on the floor and leans back against my bed. Her eyes travel over my face. "Your lip looks nasty," she observes.

Mom thinks it should have had stitches, but an EMT at the scene of the accident put some ice on it and promised it would heal up fine. "It hurts a little," I admit modestly.

"Guess you'll have to man up." Miranda smiles.

I go back to my self-portrait, knowing Miranda won't mind. "So, you heard about everything?"

"Yeah," she says. "Koby told me the whole story."

"It was a pretty bad deal."

Miranda nods. "I went and saw Ali before I came here. He's looking pretty good. In fact, he's demanding that they either discharge him or hook him up with Wi-Fi."

"Really?" That *definitely* sounds like the old Ali. "Man … that's great."

"Yeah." Miranda nods. "He'll probably go home by tomorrow."

I set down my pencil, too relieved to draw anymore. "I feel like shit about the whole thing," I admit. "I still can't believe I didn't see them. And the accident was bad enough, but then Brian turned into the Terminator... it was like a nightmare."

"And totally out of the blue like that."

Now I'm silent, knowing that isn't completely the truth. "The thing is," I tell Miranda, "Brian's been having problems since he got home. Random things happen and suddenly he thinks he's back in Afghanistan. That's what happened today, I think. Bri and I were arguing and when we hit them, well... I think the shock of it all, and the sounds and the blood... even the fact that Dr. Gabol had a scarf on his head... it must have felt to him a lot like what went on over there. The doctors said it can happen after people go through a big trauma like that... a flashback. The psychiatrist told Mom that Brian probably has post-traumatic stress disorder. Scarlett knew it before anyone else figured it out."

Scarlett. I tried to call her when I got home, but her grandma said her parents had come to town to surprise her and she was somewhere with them. I can only hope it means good things.

"So this has happened before?" Miranda asks.

"Not this bad. *Nothing* like this." As much as I want to convince her of that, I want to convince myself more. Still, I can't deny the memories of Brian's late-night neighborhood patrols, of the commands shouted in his sleep, of the pistol he slept with and hearing the words that came out of him when he shot the buck. "No," I repeat. "Nothing like this."

While Miranda and I are hanging out in my room, Mom stops by to say she's going out; the VA phoned with a list of items Brian needs for his stay, and she's running to Family Mart to pick up a few things. By the redness around her eyes, I can see she's been crying. "Did you call Dad yet?" I ask.

"Yes," she nods. "He's coming home."

The thought of Dad on his way home usually fills me with a sense of dread, but I don't feel it this time. Maybe it's because it doesn't seem like anything worse can happen.

"Do you want me to go with you?" I ask Mom. "To the store, I mean." It's suddenly occurs to me that Mom might need some company while shopping for the things her son needs for his extended stay in a psych unit. I toss the sketchpad aside. "I can do this later. Really."

Mom smiles tiredly. "Thanks, Dov," she says. "I'll be okay."

"You sure? I don't mind coming along."

She looks at me, her eyes soft. "I'm sure, sweetheart."

After she leaves, I look up to see Miranda regarding me. "That was sweet," she says. "You were worried about your mom."

I shrug. "Well," I say, "I guess I finally realized that at some point, it's not a bad idea to stop thinking just about myself. And, you know, to pay a little attention to what other people might be going through."

Miranda nods. "Yeah," she agrees. "Good idea."

My iPod is on random; *Bleed the Dream* begins to play.

"Good tunes," Miranda says, closing her eyes and tipping her head back against edge of the bed.

Sheba wanders into the doorway and stops, a question in her round golden eyes. When I don't do anything overtly threatening, she takes a tentative step across the threshold, then another. I let her come in; with Leo gone, there's no reason to keep her out. A moment later she's curled up in Miranda's lap, purring smugly.

I relax and pick up the sketchpad, returning to my drawing. After a few minutes I happen to glance up at Miranda, who's leaning back against the bed with her eyes closed, absently petting Sheba. Her red hair spikes randomly across her pale forehead, and her dark eyelashes lie against her cheeks like soft feathers. It suddenly occurs to me that she looks, well … kind of beautiful. Kind of like how she looked that night at the Poisoned Heart concert. It's a different way for me to look at Miranda, and I wonder what's changed about her to make me see her this way. Or maybe it's me … maybe *I'm* the one who's changed.

Suddenly, a question forms in my mind. "Miranda," I ask tentatively, "do you by any chance write poetry?"

Miranda's eyelashes shift and she opens her eyes. "Geez, Dov," she says with a smile that stirs the deepest part of me. "I thought you'd never ask."

(Cue loud crack as total cosmic
shift occurs in emo kid's brain)

FORTY

....

The Pepper is always busy on Saturday nights. "We thought you weren't coming." Miranda smiles, scooting over to make room for me in the booth.

"Sorry," I say. "I just got off work a half hour ago. I'm surprised I got here this quick." I slide in next to her and bump her shoulder companionably; under the table, I give her leg a quick squeeze.

Across from us, Koby rolls his eyes. "Sheesh, you two. Get a room."

Beside him, Scarlett grins. "Yeah, seriously ... you're making us sick with the PDA."

"Well, *you* won't have to put up with it much longer," I remind her. "When do you leave?"

She smiles. "Everything's packed and my parents are coming to get me in the morning."

This is our last get-together before she leaves. I'll miss Scarlett, but I'm happy for her too; she's more than ready for her family to get back to normal. I can relate.

Ali arrives a few minutes later and squeezes into the booth. "Hey," he says to me. "How's it going at the Groove?"

"Awesome," I say. "The new Poisoned Heart CD came in today and we sold out within an hour."

"Rats," he says. "You have to hook me up when the next shipment comes in."

"Absolutely." I don't tell him that he'll be finding one under the Christmas tree—one of the CDs I sold this afternoon was to Dr. Gabol, who came in to ask me how Brian was doing.

"It's been rough on him," I told Dr. Gabol honestly. "He feels awful about what happened. But I think he's getting better."

"That's good," Dr. Gabol said. "I'm happy to hear that. War, Dov, is a terrible, terrible thing."

I nodded. There was nothing more to be said.

Mom and I drive to Milford to visit Brian a couple evenings a week; Dad comes along too whenever he's home. That's where they are tonight, in fact. I had to work, so I stayed back; the Ford pickup I want isn't going to pay for itself.

Miranda nudges me. "Hey," she whispers under the buzz of our friends' conversation, "something totally amazing happened today."

"What?"

"Mrs. McGinley told me yesterday that they're going

to publish one of my poems in the *Leader*. And she wants to see my other stuff. 'Anything I've got,' she said."

"Seriously?" I exclaim, lifting an arm to wrap it around her in a hug. I've been doing a lot of that lately, and it's getting easier and easier to not feel self-conscious about it. She's my girlfriend, after all. "That's awesome, Miranda! Why didn't you tell me last night?" We talked on the phone for at least an hour; I'm surprised she didn't say anything about it.

"I wanted to see your face," she says simply.

"Well, here it is," I tell her, grinning broadly. "Look how happy it is for you!"

Miranda smiles back at me, and—I may be mistaken— I think that, for a second, the way she looks at me is an awful lot like the way Victoria used to look at Brian.

"Anyone get your grades yet?" Ali asks the table in general. "I looked mine up online this afternoon. I was sure I'd get a B in Physics, but it worked out. Thank God ... my parents would have killed me."

We all compare notes on the semester's outcome; the truth is, my report card hasn't been this good since middle school. "All B's except in art," I inform everyone. "Ms. Twohey gave me an A."

"Yeah, *duh*," Miranda laughs. "She practically rubbed Dov's self-portrait all over her body. What was that word she used again?"

"I believe it was 'pimptastic.'"

Everyone laughs as Miranda rolls her eyes. "Yeah, *that* was it."

Actually, Twohey called my self-portrait "poignant." I looked it up; it means "affecting or moving the emotions." I'm not sure that's what I was going for, but still, I'm pretty happy with how the piece turned out. At the very end, I'd decided that something was missing and impulsively spattered black ink across the image. The ink bloomed in some places and ran in others; I don't know why, but after that, it felt finished.

"I heard Twohey got engaged," Scarlett says. "Apparently the ring was an early Christmas present. She was showing off the ring in the office when I went in there to fill out my transfer papers."

"Seriously?" Miranda says.

Suddenly all my friends' eyes are on me. I lift my hands helplessly. "Look," I say, "I *told* her we should wait until I graduate, but she said if I liked it then I'd better put a ring on it..."

"You *wish*, bro," Ali says, laughing.

"So Ms. Twohey's really off the market, huh?" I sigh with pretend regret. For quite a while now, my crush on Ms. Twohey has been more of a joke than anything. I haven't even had any dreams about her for a couple weeks. That's something I actually *do* regret.

We hang out, laughing and talking together until the Pepper workers begin emptying garbage bins and making closing-up noises. There's no choice but to pack it in and reluctantly head out to the parking lot.

Koby is the first to depart. "See you in anotha life, Sistah," he says, giving Scarlett a hug. It's a line from *Lost*;

the two of them discovered a mutual passion for the show and watched re-runs of all five seasons together. In fact, I won't be surprised if I hear that there was a little *something-something* going on between them. Being marooned on a mysterious, scary island tends to do that to people.

A light snow begins to fall and Ali says his goodbyes soon after that; I suspect the medieval forests of *DarkScape* are calling his name. Now it's just the three of us.

"Well," Miranda says, giving Scarlett a hug. "Keep in touch, girl."

"I will," Scarlett promises. "And listen, keep writing, okay? Your stuff is amazing."

Miranda grins, her face flushed and happy under the streetlights. She gives me a quick hug too. "Call me later," she murmurs.

"Yep," I agree. "Soon as I get home."

Scarlett and I watch as Miranda heads off to her car. A moment later she drives past, waving at us.

"She's awesome," Scarlett says when she's gone. "I'm so happy the two of you got together."

I nod. "It's funny how you can hang out with someone every day for years, and then one day you suddenly look at them in a completely different way."

Scarlett laughs. "Miranda's been looking at you for a long time," she tells me. "I could tell the minute I got here."

"Really?"

"Yep." Scarlett smiles. "Trust me. A girl knows."

"Huh."

"Well," she says, rubbing her hands together for warmth.

"I guess I'd better take off too. I've still got a lot of stuff to pack."

"Yeah, I should get home too." Mom and Dad will be back from the VA by now, and I want to hear how Brian is doing. If everything stays on course, he could be discharged as early as next week. Of course, he'll continue his treatment as an outpatient for a long time to come.

Scarlett holds out her arms. "Hug?" she asks.

"Obviously." I squeeze her tight. "You take care of yourself," I murmur into her ear. "And I expect to see you every time you're anywhere near Longview. Not every other time... *every* time. Got it?"

Scarlett laughs, her breath warm against my cheek. "Got it."

On the street, a car rounds the corner and passes the parking lot. "EMO LOVE!!!!!!!!" screams Ray Sellers, one of his horsey laughs trailing after him.

Scarlett lets go and shakes her head. "That kid is such a tool," she sighs.

"Yeah," I agree. "You know how it is: some things change, and some are Ray Sellers."

FORTY-ONE

....

Mom is a lot more relaxed about Brian's second homecoming; no hauling of boxes, no deep cleaning of carpets, no extra measures of any kind, although she does make me go re-shovel the walk after just a light dusting of snow. "He says he wants things to be normal when he comes back this time," she says. "Not a big deal."

I, for one, am happy to oblige. Brian is excited to be coming back, although he tells me during my visit today that he's a little nervous about it too. "It just seems like everything was so nuts the last time I was home," he says.

"Well," I admit, "it *was*."

Brian sighs. "There was just too much coming at me—the media, the family, Victoria, the wedding." He shudders. "I was already on overload when I stepped off that plane, and it was all downhill from there."

I nod. After everything that's happened, it's nice to be able to just sit quietly, talking with Brian like this; nice to see signs that my brother is still in there. He says his treatment has a lot of different components: he's been attending groups to help him develop coping skills and anger management, and he's doing a lot of exercise, which is part of the treatment program too. The most important part, according to Brian, is the groups where all the veterans sit and talk about the terrible things they've seen and done. "You feel like you don't want to talk about it," Brian says, "or like you shouldn't. But getting it out … that's the only thing that helps you put it in perspective."

I think about Scarlett, and how much happier she seemed after she began talking about what had happened to her. This whole psychology thing is really starting to interest me, and I've made an appointment to talk with Mr. Kerr about his job. College applications are due soon, and Kerr says it's a good time to start exploring things like that. Not something that I ever pictured myself doing, but then again, a lot of things have changed.

"You know, Dov," Brian says as I'm getting ready to leave, "in the end, you were the one who saved me from doing something really terrible."

I shake my head. "Nah," I tell him, "the person who did that was the cop who shot the gun out of your hand." I'm only half paying attention, because I'm busy wrestling with my jacket; somehow one sleeve always ends up turned inside out.

"I'm not kidding, bro," Brian says. He waits, and when

I look up, his face is serious. "I know I was off my nut that day, but I do remember it. The one thing that stands out the most is your voice, and the way you just kept saying over and over 'you're in Longview … this is Longview.' It might not have seemed like it, but it kind of broke through, you know? Made me hesitate." Brian shakes his head. "I hate to think of what might have happened if you weren't there."

I laugh. "Well, we wouldn't have been arguing, for one thing," I remind him. "So we wouldn't have gotten in the accident, in which case I wouldn't have busted my lip open … "

Brian reaches out a hand and grips my arm. "Dov," he says. "Stop."

I shut up.

"I know this is hard for you to hear, but you're a good kid. You really grew up while I was gone. And I don't want to sound condescending, but I'm really *proud* of you. Proud to be your brother. I want you to know that."

I bite back the dismissive reply that automatically comes to my lips and make myself just accept his words.

"Even if you're a big douche," Brian adds.

"Thanks. That means a lot, coming from a mental case like you."

As I leave my brother for the time being, Scarlett's words come to mind: *Some things change, and some things stay the same,* she said.

We have all changed—Brian, Mom and Dad, Scarlett, and even me. And I realize now what I didn't before: bad situations can change people, but with a little help from each other, we can all find our way back from No Man's Land. And when we do, we're usually stronger and wiser version of ourselves.

Deep thoughts, Grasshopper. Deep thoughts indeed.

"Leo?" I exclaim, startled.

But if it is Leo, he doesn't reply. He knows I'll be okay on my own.

About Post-Traumatic Stress Disorder (PTSD)

Post-traumatic stress disorder (PTSD) is an anxiety disorder that can develop after a frightening ordeal which causes or threatens serious physical harm. Events that can generate PTSD symptoms include accidents, assaults, natural or manmade disasters, and military combat. It can occur in people regardless of age, including children and teens.

People who might develop PTSD include soldiers, rescue workers, survivors of accidents and abuse and other crimes, refugees who are fleeing violence, and the people who witness these traumatic events.

Many people with PTSD relive the frightening event again and again, through painful memories, flashbacks, or nightmares. This often occurs when they experience something that triggers memories of their ordeal. People with PTSD may also experience emotional numbness, sleep problems, depression, anxiety, intense guilt, irritability, or outbursts of anger. Most people with PTSD try to avoid things that might remind them of the original event. Depression, alcohol or other substance abuse, and other anxiety disorders frequently accompany PTSD.

Research shows that if people talk about what they went through soon after the experience, some of the symptoms of PTSD can be reduced. Also, medications such as antidepressants can help relieve the symptoms of PTSD.

Due to the number of combat veterans returning from Operation Iraqi Freedom and Operation Enduring Freedom who are experiencing symptoms of PTSD, the American Psychological Association and the National Institute of Mental Health are devoting a great deal of attention to research on this debilitating disorder.

If you know someone who is experiencing symptoms of PTSD, let them know that there is treatment that can help alleviate symptoms, and that help is available through most local mental health clinics. Veterans can access assistance for PTSD through the nearest VA clinic or treatment center.

For more information on PTSD
and/or our veterans, please consult these sites:
The National Institute of Mental Health
(http://www.nimh.nih.gov)
The United States Department of Veterans Affairs
(http://www.ptsd.va.gov)

Acknowledgments

First, thanks go to my personal special agent at Adams Literary, Quinlan Lee, for her patience, encouragement, perseverance, business acumen, and North Carolina charm. Thanks to Flux editors Brian Farrey-Latz, for his enthusiasm and guidance on our first venture together, and Sandy Sullivan, for having the eyes of an eagle and the best "tweaks" around. Thanks to Adrienne Zimiga and Bob Gaul for knowing just how to represent the story visually and for patiently entertaining my ideas, and big thanks to Anastasia Scott and Alisha Bjorklund for getting the word out about *No Man's Land*.

Thank you to Gayle Stordahl for your fierce copyediting skills, honed on each morning's edition of the *Grand Forks Herald*. I've got you on speed dial. Thanks also to the Red Pepper, a Grand Forks institution, for providing inspiration and great food. Readers, if you've never had a grinder from the Pepper, well… get there! And thank you, Miranda Langevin, for the rabid chipmunk impersonation. I promised that if you showed it to me, I'd name a character after you, and I always keep my promises.

A shout-out to the original Tribes (now known as Paramount) for inspiring me with your music and stage presence. Your shows gave me a front-row view into the hardcore music scene (and a bruise once, when I got too near the mosh pit.) A wink and a thank-you to Jack McGinley and Doug Stangeland for their contributions to *No Man's Land*. Good thing you guys know the classics like you do.

Many thanks also to my entire Facebook cheering section for the support and encouragement you offered during the writing process. Susan Thompson Underdahl LIKES this.

Endless gratitude to my husband, Shane, and to Navy, Fiona, Beck, Alexa, Chloe, and Jaiden for being my steady source of support, inspiration, love, and laughter. Special thanks to my own in-house illustrator, Beck Thompson, for bringing Dov's artwork to life on my website. I'd love to work together again in the future, especially if you continue to let me pay you in video games.

And finally, thank you, gentle readers, especially when you take the time to write or email to let me know how my books affect you. You make it all worthwhile.

About the Author

Susan Thompson Underdahl is a North Dakota native who likes to believe she does not have any trace of a Midwestern accent. She once had an eight-year friendship with a ghost, and she can occasionally breathe underwater, but not on command. During the weekdays, she is a neuropsychologist specializing in the evaluation and treatment of dementia and brain injury. On evenings and weekends, she is the keeper of one daughter, two sons, and three stepdaughters, in addition to two cats, two dogs, and one husband. On her lunch hours, she writes.

Visit Susan online at www.stunderdahl.com.